Stolen Sunshine

A Woman's Quest for Herself

....the veil did not only hide the woman's face, it systematically segregated her from the outside world, and also the changes and the progress around her. The veil was symbolic of her cocooned status, her helplessness....

....women are educating themselves, there is virtually no field they have not excelled in. They have emerged from their veiled confines and are facing the world with confidence.

The desire to win under any circumstances, determination to overcome all odds, the courage to face adversity, and to tread on less travelled roads led Rukmini to attain untouched heights of success and a place in the society.

Stolen Sunshine

A Woman's Quest for Herself

SMITA JHAVAR

New Age Books

New Age Books

ISBN: 81-7822-080-6

First Edition: 2002

Published by
NEW AGE BOOKS
A-44 Naraina Phase I
New Delhi-110 028 (INDIA)
Email: nab@vsnl.in
Website: www.newagebooksindia.com

Printed in India
by Jainendra Prakash Jain at Shri Jainendra Press
A-45 Naraina Phase-I New Delhi-110 028

To My Parents,
For accepting me with all my faults
and still believing in me.
For loving me like no one else in the world
ever did or will ever do.

To My Masi, Rukmini
Whose indomitable spirit inspired me
to write this book.

Contents

Acknowledgements

I am indebted to each of my well-wishers who have encouraged me in their own special way.

My brother Prakash, for being my severest critic, (not only for this book but always) which however makes me put in my best.

My husband Sudarshan for his silent encouragement, that is, by not interfering at all!

My children Swasti and Suvrat who were more excited about the book than I was.

With their arrival the word 'responsibility' took on a new meaning, and it is also because of them that I got an insight into the depth of relationships, and realized that my parents love me unconditionally.

My niece Pragya for patiently putting my manuscript in order, and seeing me through those dreadful wriggly red and green lines on the computer screen.

Rajendra, Ravi and Rajeev for their reassurance, guidance and encouragement in bringing out the book. I am indeed fortunate to have such wonderful friends.

Alka and Jeetendra, who have contributed so much to my thought process, and have always been such great supports.

Kishorebhai, for helping me with the research.

Mr. V.G. Andurkar's book 'Solapur Martial Law Ani Char Hutatma' which I have used for historical facts.

Last but not least. I am thankful to Shri R.K. Mehra of Rupa Publications for kindly going through the MSS and making useful suggestions.

SMITA JHAVAR

Introduction

I am a Marwari and proud to be one. But it was not always so. So often, in school I evaded answering the question we still can't help asking each other, "What are you?" I would say I am a Rajasthani, and deliberately refrained from being more specific. Marwaris had the stigma of being extremely thrifty, and I chose to avoid it as much as I could help.

As I grew up and my understanding matured, my perception about our community gradually changed. I was now able to see the strengths of a hard working and a proud people. Gifted with a sharp intellect and quick reflexes, Marwaris are a lot determined to face and overcome all odds. The desire to win under any circumstances gives them tremendous risk taking abilities and unbelievable guts. They are fortunate to inherit from their forefathers the willingness to struggle and work hard.

Religion and business have dominated Marwari homes for centuries and still continue to do so. Men rarely adhere to strict business hours, and work relentlessly. Still they are very family oriented. Family does not mean one's wife and children but it extends to grand parents, uncles, aunts, nieces, nephews, often staying together and for whom they feel equally responsible. Marwaris are disciplined, bound by values and tradition and deeply religious. Perhaps these very traits bog them down sometimes. I grew up seeing the talents, intelligence and strengths of Marwari women go unrecognized and underestimated primarily because they were uneducated and unexposed to the world outside. Sadly, they were also greatly misunderstood by others. They were seen as women who could not think beyond their homes, hearth and children and whose interests were limited to clothes and jewellery. Their intelligence was always doubted and it pained me deeply.

The scenario has changed drastically now. As Marwari women are educating themselves, there is virtually no field they have not excelled in. They have emerged from their veiled confines and are facing the world with confidence like any other women of the world.

This book is a tribute to their triumph.

February 2002 SMITA JHAVAR

I

Kesar Maa : 1914

It was 3.30 in the morning when Kesar maa descended from the second floor of her *haveli* to the ground floor where the well was. She put a *diya* in a glass box and held it up with its handle to illuminate the dark stairway.

It was *Kartik* and the temperatures had dipped. But every year during *Kartik* she would bathe before it was dawn and then attend to her *puja* and daily chores. "*Shree Krishna Sharnam Mama*" was like breath to her. It sustained and rejuvenated her. She chanted it, in every moment of her waking hour.

Chanting it now she dropped the canvas bag into the well and pulled up icy cold water. Slowly she filled a copper container broad at the top and narrow at the bottom. She bathed recalling the names of all the holy rivers—*Ganga, Yamuna, Saraswati, Krishna, Kaveri*...

With hair still dripping, she wrapped herself in an off-white silk sari and headed straight for the *puja-ghar* where her Gopal was still sleeping. The droplets dripping from her hair formed an unpredictable pattern on the stone stairs as she climbed up.

Every day at the crack of dawn she would wake him up with *Mangala Aarti* but not before she had prepared breakfast of fresh *pedhas, barfi* or *rabdi* with thickened milk. Her Gopal would be hungry after a long winter night. After the waking ritual, Gopal would be bathed and dressed in the finest of clothes made of rich velvet, satin, silk or then cotton, depending upon the weather. After the *Bhog Aarti*, Gopal would rest and Kesar maa would have a little warm milk.

It was already 6 O'clock now and Kesar maa was in a hurry today. Her three and a half-year-old daughter was to be engaged in the auspicious hour of the morning. She hurried to the kitchen where the house helps, the cooks and the maids were already busy. Kesar maa was so engrossed that she never realised when her daughter Radha entered the kitchen and put her arms around her.

"Radha!" Kesar maa nearly screamed, "Why did you enter the kitchen before bathing? You have touched me too. I'll have to change my clothes now."

Radha wouldn't let go. All she needed was some attention, but her mother was too busy to give her that. A maid tried to pull her away, but Radha held a corner of her mother's sari in protest.

"Please Radha. I have so much work to do. The guests will be here in a few hours."

She called for the maid. "Take her away, get her ready, make her wear the pink silk frock."

Radha retreated, her faced flushed with anger and hurt.

Radha was to be engaged to nine-year-old Girdhar, who lived in a mansion across the street. He was the only son of the family. Their mansion was decorated with Italian marble and Belgian glass in golden frames. From the ceiling hung the chandeliers from England. The heavy Burmese teakwood almirahs were engraved with intricate grapevines, parrots and peacocks. The mansion had a central courtyard with a fountain. All around were rooms. The ground floor catered to the men. They sat on milky white cotton sheets spread on thick mattresses. The walls were lined with bolsters on which the men reclined and talked. On one side business transactions were conducted by managers and accounts managed by trusted *munims*. Opposite this area was a wooden staircase which led to the second floor. This was the women's domain. There the women could sit unveiled. Behind the common halls were the bedrooms.

The second floor housed the kitchen dominated mainly by the head cook or *maharaj* and the women folk. He had a group of helpers under him.

The women supervised the overall functioning of the kitchen, but rarely did the actual cooking.

Girdhar's home also hummed with a flurry of activity. Girdhar was aware that he was going to be engaged to Radha. He didn't understand what engagement meant but he enjoyed the attention he received because of it. He got a new silk *sherwani* and *dhoti*. He wore an emerald and pearl necklace around his neck. Pearl drops adorned his small ears. He shook his head consciously so that they dangled delicately.

"Aren't you going to play with Radha today?" Somebody had teased him.

He couldn't figure out what was so different today. He had played with Radha whenever his father carried her on his shoulders and brought her home. She would hold his orange turban for balance and he would hold his daughter-in-law's tiny feet. He loved to hear her silver anklet bells tinkle. She was the daughter he never had. People smiled at the sight.

"You will spoil her," some would say. She would come and play with Girdhar for hours.

Girdhar heard his father Jagannath call out.

"Aren't the women ready yet? The *muhurt* time is drawing near."

Jagannath looked regal in a white *sherwani* and crisp white *dhoti*. He wore a brand new starched orange *pagdi*. Gold buttons shone brightly, encrusted with pea sized rubies. He opened the big iron safe and removed jewellery for Radha and carefully placed it on a silver platter. Small gold bangles, tiny earrings, a gold waist band trimmed with *ghungroos*, a small *jadau bor* to adorn her head, a variety of necklaces and chokers, small anklets with tiny tinkling bells and rings to fit Radha's small podgy fingers.

Jagannath had ordered the goldsmith to work at home and he had personally supervised the crafting of each piece of jewellery. He hadn't trusted anybody because he wanted small sizes of everything. Nothing would be sent for his *bahu* that was oversized. All he asked his wife to make were small frocks for Radha. So dozens of frocks in finest material and trimmed with pure gold *gota* and silver *zardozi* were stitched for her.

Jagannath reclined on one of the bolsters, waiting for the women to descend. He looked at the stained glass semicircular ventilators adorning the windows and doors. The sunlight came in, reflecting patterns and colours on the white sheets.

The road to success and this grandeur hadn't been easy. Goddess Lakshmi had smiled on them, but after a long struggle.

How could he forget that burdened childhood? Fruitlessly toiling on a stubborn piece of desert land in Rajasthan. The angry sun mercilessly spat fire on his father who tilled the land in hope of a *bajra* crop, which would feed his family. But again God Indra would fail them. The clouds came and went away without showering their benevolence and making the already grim faces grimmer. It became increasingly difficult for his father Ramsukh to face the blank hungry faces of his mother, wife and children. Drinking water was scarce and his wife walked one mile every day to fill pitchers of drinking water from a drying well. Water which flowed after bathing would be collected in a pit. This was used for washing clothes.

There was no respite from difficulties, which came upon them one after the other. They were tired of living such a difficult and tough life where survival posed new challenges every day.

Steadily there was migration from the whole of Rajasthan. Male members left their homes leaving behind their wives and children and migrated to earn a livelihood. They spread throughout India from big cities to the tiny villages, any place where they could earn a living and send some money back home. They took on all sorts of jobs, as labourers, tailors, carpenters, cooks, salesmen, and accountants, anything that would give them a livelihood with dignity. Nobody ever begged. As they prospered, more were encouraged to leave their homes for greener pastures.

Rajasthan was known as Marwar then and people who hailed from there were known as Marwaris. They fanned out all over India, merging with the local people, learning their language, speaking their tongue, imbibing their customs, but at the same time guarding their distinct identity.

More and more young people got their families to live with them but they retained their traditions, values and dress code. This was a community that had faced immense hardship, experienced poverty and hunger. So when they prospered they saved every anna they earned. They saved to send money to their families back home, they saved to set up businesses of their own. They saved for a secure future for their children and to build homes for them in an alien land. But with it they acquired the social stigma of being thrifty or *kanjoos*. It would take centuries to shake this stigma off their backs.

Ramsukh decided to leave Marwar for prosperity. He was not alone though. A few of his friends agreed to join him. He left home with Rs. 5 in his pocket, *sattu* made by his mother (it was a mixture of gram flour, ghee and sugar) an earthen pot of drinking water, dreams in his eyes and a will to succeed. His heart remained in Marwar though.

It was the late 19th century. The whole of India was awakening to join the freedom struggle against the British. Ramsukh and his friend (who would be Radha's grandfather) decided to settle in Solapur, a small, dusty town known for its thriving cotton business in Maharashtra in western India. The rest had settled in other places. Ramsukh sympathised with the freedom fighters but never got involved with active politics. His aim was only to earn money.

The only investment they had was hard work. Ramsukh found a job in a cloth merchant's shop. His job involved carrying the cloth bales on his shoulders and selling them in town. He earned a commission on the cloth he sold. His employer would feed him in the afternoons. The dinner was simple, puffed rice, gram jaggery and peanuts. He missed the *bajra* or *jo rotis* his mother made for him. He had to eat *jowar rotis* here to which he was not accustomed.

When a delicate hand touched the cottons he sold, he missed his wife. When a child clung to his mother, he thought of his son Jagannath. But he found consolation in the fact that the money he was sending would not let them go hungry.

He slept on a thin *chatai* weaving dreams. How elegant his wife would look in a *ghagra* made from this fine English material. Someday she would sit in a haveli, playing *chopad*; she would have servants to work for her. And his mother wouldn't have to grind any more. Jagannath would be fed milk, butter and ghee. He would go to school and play with his friends instead of working in the fields. Ramsukh would drift off to sleep, resting his tired body to face a hard day ahead.

His hard work and honesty bore fruits. His employer was pleased with the increasing sales and he was put in charge of the whole shop. He now received a comfortable salary. He would be the first one to arrive at the shop and the last one to leave. He left only after tallying the daily accounts.

The shop now had a changed look. The white sheets were bleached and cloth bales were stacked neatly. He kept the accounts meticulously; accounting for each anna spent and earned.

Ramsukh knew the knack of keeping the staff happy. He helped them financially in case of illness or marriages. He sent their children sweets on Holi and Diwali and got new clothes for them on special occasions. He gave them a bonus when their firm made a profit. They were prepared to work harder for him.

After two years of hard work, Ramsukh asked for a partnership in the shop. Mumbai harbour had become an important business centre. He purchased a shop at Kalbadevi and employed a Marwari *munim*. Cloth arrived straight from England and was loaded in trains to reach Solapur. Ramsukh was the first to import cloth from England and his shop thrived because of the growing demand for English cloth. Ramsukh could now think of expanding his business.

Ramsukh brought his family to Solapur. The farm in Rajasthan was sold and the house locked. He built a house here and later a mansion. When he died, he had already trained Jagannath to handle the business.

The wooden staircase made a soft drumming sound as the women descended from the first floor. It broke Jagannath's reverie and they proceeded to Radha's home for the engagement ceremony.

Jagannath was smiling. His daughter-in-law was indeed beautiful. Eyes large and expressive, thick eyelashes that touched her eyebrows, black curly hair, framing her fair cherubic face. But what charmed him was her sweet tinkling voicc. She, unaware that she was talking to her father-in-law, sat on his lap and chattered while the *pundit* performed the *puja.*

II
Radha : 1920

Kesar maa was worried. Radha was nine, old enough to be married. Before people started talking, she decided that a marriage date ought to be fixed. She had already broached the subject with her husband but he hadn't taken it very seriously.

Kesar maa had no child after Radha. It did worry them sometimes, that there was no inheritor, no one to carry on the family name, but Kesar maa had accepted the fact as one of her 'Gopal's wish'. They were no one to question his *marji.*

Oh! Gopal must be hungry. He hadn't had anything to eat since lunch. She stirred some almonds, sugar, saffron in warm milk and placed the silver bowl before Gopal. She pulled a silk curtain before him. Her Gopal ate and drank behind a curtain, away from evil eyes that would harm his delicate constitution. Just then Radha entered, rubbing her sleepy eyes and sat on her mother's lap. Kesar maa smoothened Radha's curly hair off her forehead and encircled her small face with her palms.

"Maa I am hungry."

"Just a moment the milk in the *Bhog* is ready, I have put lots of almonds today. Come, I'll pull the curtain and..."

Kesar maa hadn't finished saying yet when Radha interrupted her sharply "Maa, why do you give me Gopal's *jhoota* milk every day, why don't you ever make milk only for me? The food you make, the *laddus* the *rabdi, pedhas*, every thing, just everything is his *jhoota* and I am telling you, I won't eat a thing offered to him first. I'll eat what you make only for me."

It wasn't Radha's temperament to get angry. She was a happy child, so Kesar maa was taken by surprise. She thought of something to say, but before that Radha continued...

"You stitch his clothes first and decorate it with *gota.*"

Angrily pointing at the drawn curtain, she said, "It's him you fan the whole day in summer and warm him with a silver stove in winter. You celebrate his birthday each year but you don't ever remember my birthday." Kesar maa still looked on disbelievingly at Radha.

Radha thumped to the curtain and pulled it aside. There was Gopal sitting on a maroon velvet cushion smiling mischievously. It made Radha angrier. Perpetually sitting in a crawling stance, one palm raised to hold a round *laddu*, he commanded all her mother's attention. The small gold crown, encrusted with red and white stones glistened. A tilted peacock feather was tucked carefully in the crown. Radha knew the long hours her mother spent in adorning Gopal while she was dressed by the maids.

"He doesn't move from his velvet throne, but you love him more than you love me."

Radha couldn't stop crying. Tears melted Kesar maa's heart, but no amount of consoling quietened Radha. She refused to drink milk or eat anything. It was evening by then. Kesar maa quietly walked up to Gopal. It was time for the evening *aarti*. She dipped the wick in *ghee* and carefully placed it in the silver *diya*, lighted it and closed her eyes with palms joined together in *namaskar*.

Radha looked on in silence, terribly hurt.

Everybody at home was now talking about Radha's marriage. All she could make out of it was that she would have to leave her home and live at Girdhar's mansion. It didn't worry her much though. She had no companion here and could play with him at least, but she was forbidden to visit his place these days. Occasionally when she did go she was draped in a six-yard sari that had to be folded into half so as to make it her size. The numerous folds made her look fat at the stomach and also made her gait funny. Girdhar laughed at her and teased her. Radha didn't like it at all, but she had been warned not to talk to him any more, so she forced herself not to protest.

Radha enjoyed the attention Maa and Baba gave her. Baba, as she called her father had shopped for her in Mumbai. He had bought the finest of brocades, silks and mulmuls and Maa had a tailor right at home who worked from morning till evening stitching *ghagras*, *cholis* and petticoats. Plain cloth was embellished with pure gold and silver sequins and *zari*. She loved it when she was summoned to try on her new clothes. Radha wore her *ghagras* and went round and round in circles, squatting when the skirt was all around her. She danced before the large mirrors to hear the tinkle of her jewellery. Radha laughed, enthralled by her own performance.

To her surprise, everybody seemed to listen to what she had to say. Nobody ignored her any more and it made her chatter even more. She was the star. Women sang around her and none of her friends got angry with her. She was pleased at the way they made her win all the games each time. Marriage was tremendous fun, she thought.

Daily massage, herbal treatments and *mehendi* applications were enjoyable, but most of all she revelled in the attention she received.

Nine and a half-year-old Radha was married to fifteen-year-old Girdhar. When it was time for the main ceremony both were fast asleep. They were exhausted by the end of the day. Rituals performed all day long drained them of their energy. Radha was sleeping peacefully in Kesar maa's bedroom when she was brought to the *mandap* for the *pheras*.

She slept throughout the ceremony, while Girdhar tried his best to stay awake. The warmth of the *hawan* and the droning sound of the *mantras* recited by the *pundit* had a tranquillising effect, which was difficult to fight. But he wanted to behave like a man and didn't want to sleep like his bride.

Radha left with her groom. Kesar maa felt as if a part of her had gone away. What was it that had been amputated? Her heart? Her spirit? She didn't know, but she felt incomplete and insecure. Some consoled her saying Radha hadn't gone far off, just across the street. She could see her whenever she felt like. But Kesar maa knew her only daughter was no longer hers.

That day Radha slept in her mother-in-law's bedroom. She felt suffocated in the veil. The *odhna* was pulled over her face to form the veil, through which she couldn't see clearly. She was yet to master the art of lifting the veil with the fingers to see the world outside, without exposing any part of the face. If that was not enough she was taught over and over again by Kesar maa not to talk to anyone, never to laugh loudly, never to sleep or eat unless asked to do so. When the suffocation was unbearable, she had sneaked into her mother-in-law's room.

A smile lit Jamna's face when she entered her room and saw Radha. Her left palm was under her chubby left cheek as she slept on her side. The *odhna* with which Radha had managed to cover herself the whole day lay near her crumpled in a small heap. Her *ghagra* had hitched up to reveal her small feet and smooth fair calves. The *mehendi* had coloured her feet a deep maroon and the small silver anklets shone brighter on it. She had slept with her jewellery on, too afraid to remove it. Girdhar's mother removed her heavy gold *kadas* and necklace and pulled her *ghagra* down to her feet.

She realised then how beautiful her daughter-in-law was.

The angel-like cherubic face was content and peaceful in deep sleep. It must have been so difficult for Kesar maa to part with her, Jamna thought. For the first time she did not regret not having a daughter. At least she was spared from the pain of parting with one's own flesh and blood.

Just then Jagannath entered his bedroom, saw Radha sleeping there, smiled at his wife and left in search of a quiet place in the busy household where he could rest for the night.

III
Girdhar-Radha

Radha's marriage was the end of her childhood. It slowly shrivelled as restrictions were imposed upon her. She was constantly reminded that she was now married and so 'grown up'.

She ought to walk slowly and not prance about. Laughing and talking loudly were bad manners. Too much gesticulating while talking wasn't good etiquette. A girl should talk with her hands stationary and eyes down. Even Kesar maa was 'training' her to be a good daughter-in-law, because a daughter's behaviour reflected how the mother had groomed the girl.

Every bit of Radha rebelled, but slowly the fire in her quietened. Now there was dumb acceptance. The bubbly Radha mellowed and grew quiet. She made herself believe that it was now time to stop playing with friends and to assume household responsibilities.

Time flies fast. Radha was thirteen, but a lot happened in these three and a half years. Her father died. Kesar maa was just twenty-eight years old. To overcome her grief, she had taken refuge in Gopal. She spent more and more time in prayer. Radha became lonelier. She couldn't bear the sight of her mother in a plain white cotton sari and no jewellery except for two gold bangles. But Kesar maa's face was still luminous. For inexplicable reasons, the grief had not managed to dim its brightness.

It reflected peace and not the turmoil within. She still looked beautiful. Her stunning beauty often reminded Radha of the times when Baba was alive.

Baba had been ill for a long time now. *Vaids* and English

doctors administered everything, from ayurvedic to *angrezi* medicine. Nothing helped his failing health. A doctor then suggested a change in climate and environment.

Baba agreed to go to Mahabaleshwar. It was at a distance of 250 kms away from Solapur and was known for its unpolluted therapeutic climate. Kesar maa had packed for days on end. Food would be cooked at the bungalow they had rented. So utensils and stoves, grains and *masalas* were packed.

Her Gopal was prepared for the journey too. In went his clothes and silver utensils, his velvet cushions and other paraphernalia. Gopal travelled in a silver filigree basket.

Radha was very excited because it was the first time she would leave Solapur. She was glad to get a break from her restrictions as a *bahu*. The party left with a servant, a maid and a cook.

Radha loved the hills. She roamed the small pathways by foot or on a pony hired for her. She picked *jamuns* that fell with a thud on the ground and splattered a bright purple on the soft red mud. She discovered that the ones, which splattered, were the sweetest. Radha filled them in cones she made from Banyan leaves. She washed them and ate them till her tongue, lips and teeth were all stained purple. She stuck her tongue out repeatedly to see how deep the colour was. Obviously Kesar maa reprimanded her for this unladylike act.

Mainly the English visited Mahabaleshwar. They retreated to the hills to beat the hot Indian summer. It was the first time Radha saw the English at such close quarters. She watched with curiosity their mannerisms, their way of dressing and the ease with which their women moved about. She had never seen women mingle so freely with men and it intrigued her. She was also stunned to see the women wear skirts that revealed their bare legs, and wide necked dresses that showed their backs and fronts generously. She wondered how their mothers allowed them to dress so outrageously. But what left her shocked and shaken was a boat ride at the lake. The boat man had gone some distance and then stopped, allowing the three to breathe in fresh air and feel the breeze on their faces. Kesar maa's sari had been blown off her head, and for the first time Radha had seen her mother unconscious of it. She let her *palla* fly behind her and strands of hair across her face. Radha had lowered her hand in the serene water and splashed it.

Just then another boat came up. She saw an English couple entwined in each other's arms, faces close together, kissing, touching.

Radha had never seen anyone behaving so peculiarly.

Baba and Maa. . . they rarely spoke in her presence. The only time she saw them hold hands in public was during her marriage. The *pundit* had put Maa's hand in Baba's, for the *kanyadaan*. When both had given her away, as a bride to Girdhar. With 'Agni Devta' or the Fire God as the witness to the ceremony.

Her father-in-law and mother-in-law rarely looked at one another. Spouses were ignored during conversations according to joint family norms. Girdhar and her. . . . She closed her eyes. . . .

She didn't want to look at her parents' reaction, but still when she opened her eyes she was looking at them.

Baba looked away, lips pursed.

Maa had lowered her eyes into her lap, red faced. Then she collected the flying sari end around her head and shoulders, shrinking back into its safety and sanctity.

Baba had regained some strength and was feeling more enthusiastic. He went for long walks with Kesar maa and Radha by his side.

On one such walk a group of young English officers crossed their paths. They sensed they were stared at and Kesar maa lowered her eyes. One of the officers said loudly, "Didn't I tell you that woman was beautiful? They live in the bungalow down the road. I watch her every day during her walks."

He had assumed that nobody would understand English. Kesar maa and Radha didn't, but Radha's father had learnt English as he dealt with many English businessmen. His face reddened with anger, as he watched them pass, staring and laughing. "How did you miss the girl, man?" Another one replied, "she's as beautiful and untouched too."

Kesar maa saw her husband brooding that day. As they finished their dinner, he had announced loudly so that the servants would hear too.

"Pack up everything, we will leave as soon as we are ready."

Kesar maa begged to know the reason.

"You have just started regaining your strength, you ought to stay here for some more time," she had implored.

But his decision remained unchanged and they returned to Solapur. Baba had never improved after that. Slowly his health deteriorated and he died leaving behind a young widow and a large flourishing business.

Radha now lived more with her in-laws, and Kesar maa was left alone with her Gopal. He gave her life a direction and also a meaning to live. He motivated her towards *dharma* and she was inspired to donate large amounts to temples and guest houses, feed and clothe Brahmins, give alms and clothe the poor.

She was fortunate to have *munims* who believed that it was their duty to carry on the business with absolute honesty and integrity even after their *sethji's* death. The highest paid *munim* in their firm received a salary of Rs.200 per year, while he made a profit of lakhs of rupees for his employer. He was proud to be the most trusted *munim* to a most pious lady. He discussed business only once with Kesar maa—at the end of the financial year. He would inform her of the profits her business had made. She would nod, her face hidden behind the white cotton sari. The only other time he met her was when Kesar maa needed large amounts of money for donations or some religious purposes, otherwise, there was rarely any interaction between them.

Kesar maa asked him for the sum and *Munimji* never refused. Money for the household expenses was sent at the beginning of each month with which Kesar maa ran the household.

This was an era where money did give a person a social status but it was also an era where elders were respected. Sometimes only for the simple reason that they had a greater number of years to their credit. No other qualification was really necessary.

The elders governed the personal, social and economic lives of the youngsters to a great extent. Any rebels were resented and looked down upon by the family. One could only wait to grow old till he could run his life and revel in the taste of intoxicating power.

IV

Radha And Krishna : 1927

Fourteen-year-old Radha was aware of most of her duties and responsibilities by now. She knew she had to be present when *papads* were rolled and dried, when mangoes were pickled or when sacks of grain were sifted, cleaned and stored. Most of the time she just watched doing nothing. But she knew her presence was necessary. She couldn't disappear when her mother-in-law worked or when women came to help make chips. The long, hot afternoons made her drowsy but she sat through all the ordeals. Slowly she learnt the recipes of pickles and how the dough for *papad* was pounded. She learnt to cut the dough with a thread so that the balls retained their round shape. A knife would flatten the dough so she learnt how to tie a sturdy thread to her big toe and slice the long rope-like dough with the thread.

But sometimes the child in her wanted her to stop being a woman. She just wanted to stop pretending and play.

The courtyard looked like a massive chessboard with black and white Italian marble squares. Whenever she had to cross the courtyard she hopped on the white squares and skipped the black. She hitched up her *ghagra* with both hands and jumped, her anklets tinkling. Sometimes she stopped suddenly; scared she would be seen playing around. She hid her skipping rope in her cupboard and skipped whenever she was alone.

The *naayan* came every week to wash and oil her hair. She would braid and plait it tightly. A heavy, encrusted *bor* was then adorned on her head, which was only removed the following week. Radha didn't like the massage she gave with *besan* and *malai*. Though it left her skin glistening and smooth, it hurt when the hair on her arms and legs were pulled. The *naayan* dipped a soft cotton sari in a solution of water and a liberal sprinkle of saffron. This scented garment Radha wore at night. It pleased the husband's senses, she was told.

Still she waited for the *naayan's* arrival each week. Radha was excused that day from the daily chores and she cajoled the lady to play *chopad*, *chirmi* or *pachkuta*. For a day she became a child and she tried to salvage some of her lost childhood.

Girdhar now nineteen and a half had left school and joined his father in business. Jagannath had explained to him one day, "Girdhar it's time you left school. After all you don't have to do a job or become a *babu.*"

"A Marwari is fit to join his family business the day he knows how to calculate interest and compound interest. You shouldn't waste your time, studying more history or geography. It's time you understood your business now."

Girdhar thought his father was right and he left school without any regrets. His father speculated a great deal in cotton. He saw his father making a lot of money or sometimes losing heavily. But he soon picked up the tricks of his father's trade and Jagannath was proud of his son's business acumen.

He kept a close watch on Girdhar's activities though. He couldn't invest or spend without his or Laduramji's permission. Laduram was Jagannath's most trusted *munim* and manager. He controlled the finances and nothing could be done without his assent. It was imperative for Girdhar to consult Laduramji before he took any financial decisions. Girdhar's suggestions could be rejected outright by him without so much as a question from Girdhar. On rare occasions, he asked for explanations, which Laduramji had the privilege not to give.

Girdhar's major distraction was Radha. She ignored him and resisted his attempts to draw her attention towards him. Her innocent beauty attracted him, but whenever he tried to hold her hand or touch her cheeks, she jingled her anklets and bangles to create a small noise. Girdhar withdrew lest someone heard. Radha took the opportunity to run away. She would leave him in dismay and go away to Kesar maa for days and days.

"God! How would she ever understand?" he would ask his married friends.

"Oh! Don't worry, she'll understand as soon as you share your bedroom with her." They laughed.

What she understood or what she didn't was irrelevant. Fourteen-year-old Radha conceived and the whole household rejoiced. Denied of her own childhood, she was not mature enough to understand what motherhood meant. Fear gripped her, as she didn't know what was in store for her. Her mental burden was no less than her increasing physical burden and she didn't know whom to turn to.

She was too embarrassed to ask Kesar maa for anything. Girdhar seemed as ignorant as her. He was unable to solve her numerous doubts. He said he didn't know what happened at childbirth, or what she should expect.

"Oh! Then why didn't you ask your friends to educate you fully? You learnt only what suited you. You don't have to worry about anything now, do you?" Radha was intentionally sarcastic. Girdhar still had no answer.

The only person she could think of was Pushkarbai who had sired seven children herself. 'Pusibai' as she was called was a Brahmani who helped the *maharaj* in the kitchen.

It was afternoon and the house was quiet. Radha reached the kitchen on the top floor and found the *maharaj* relaxing, smoking a *bidi*. His thick knotty legs emerged straight before him from a pot that was his belly. The *janeu* or the sacred cotton thread crossed his chest, and went taut over his belly. He had a moustache he was immensely proud of. Whenever he could, he stiffened it with his thumb and forefinger till it pointed sharply upwards. He had keen, alert eyes sheltered by thick, bushy eyebrows. His head was shaven but for the *choti,* which he tied in a small, neat knot. The *maharaj* had been employed in the family for twenty years now and the women and other servants had no choice but to respect him. Very often, his impudence had to be overlooked.

He saw Radha, but chose to ignore her. He disliked his quiet afternoons being intruded upon and she did not dare to disturb him.

The kitchen smelt differently at different times. Early in the morning it smelt of the incense Pusibai lighted before a few photographs of various deities. Then as the cook lit the firewood to feed the *choolah* it smelt of smoke and charcoal. Watery eyed and coughing he proceeded to cook the meal. The appetising aroma of ghee and spluttering mustard, the tangy smell of fresh coriander *chutney* ground on stone, the smell of fresh *rotis* turning into fluffy balls filled the kitchen. Now it smelt of wet mud.

The *choolah* was freshly coated with it, ash cleared from its belly. It could rest till the fires would be lit again for the evening cooking.

Radha loved the various smells and the memories associated with it. The wet *choolah* reminded her of the first shower of rain and its earthy smell.

The clang of vessels being cleaned broke the silence of the lazy afternoon.

Pusibai held a brass *katori* in her palm, which contained a little ash from the *choolah*. She pinched some and rubbed it on her eyebrows. Radha was amused.

Pusibai must have been quite attractive when younger, Radha thought. She wasn't beautiful, but something in her face was interesting and attractive. It made one look at her again.

She had a strong, square jaw and a slim face. Her eyes were dark and expressive. Though she bore seven children, she had a slender, flat-stomached body.

The only thing that gave her age away were her breasts. Stitched clothes were not allowed in the kitchen while cooking, so she never wore a blouse. Sometimes, the *pallav* of her sari would slip to reveal a pair of shrivelled, sagging breasts. As if these didn't belong to the body, they hung on. They didn't match.

"What exactly are you doing, Pusibai?"

"Making my eyebrows shapely. If you rub the extra hair with ash it gets pulled out. See my eyebrows are like a perfect bow. You could do it too, want to get it done?" she asked, not even looking away from the small mirror she held in her hand.

"*Na baba*, it hurts doesn't it?"

Pusibai smiled a crooked smile. One side of her lips smiling a little more than the other. Her eyes narrowed as she spoke to Radha.

She was looking at Radha now.

"My princess, you'll know what pain is when you get your baby."

Pusibai had hit the nail on the head. This was exactly what Radha feared most. The fear she had been concealing till now was now all over her innocent face. Scared and vulnerable, she hated herself for looking thus. So she quickly collected her scattered nerves.

"Where does it hurt? Is it so unbearable? You've had so many children. You bore the pain too. Will my pain be greater than yours? All women go through this don't they?"

Questions tumbled out of her like gushing water from a halted dam.

Pusibai melted a little. She took pity on the scared Radha. She held Radha's soft hands in her rough hardened ones.

"Don't worry *beta*, we'll look after you very well. Why do you worry? The almighty has given us women a large share of pain and suffering, but he has also given us the strength to bear it. You will forget all the pain when you see your first-born. You will want to hold and feed the infant, you will..." Radha cut her short.

"So many women die when they have babies. Will I die too?"

"No my child, no," Pusibai convinced her, "Only those

women die who are not looked after well. That can't happen to you, can it? Kesar maa will look after you very well."

That was the only excuse she could think of and it seemed to work. Radha calmed down. Within a few minutes she was learning the finer details of shaping eyebrows. For some time at least she forgot to fear the future.

Children have this invaluable gift of living in the present. Their past does not intrude the tranquillity of the present and nor do their minds prey on the uncertainties of the future. A child celebrates the present, lives in it to the full, and so is always happy. A broken toy, a scolding from mother, leaves him unhappy, but for only a while. In no time the toy is forgotten, and something else occupies his little mind. Happiness engulfs him once again, he is not worried about another scolding either.

Radha was but a child, forced into adulthood.

Radha went away to stay with Kesar maa, in the last days of her pregnancy. Those last difficult days and the labour pain, Radha bore it all with quiet dignity. She was learning not to protest, not to ask questions. She was becoming an ideal daughter and *bahu.*

Radha gave birth to a baby girl. Jagannath celebrated it with such great zeal that people were surprised. A first-born that was a girl was not a matter to celebrate. It was more a time to console the family. First daughters bring good luck and wealth was the most common one used to console the family. When Radha's daughter was born not a single servant was willing to go and announce her birth to Jagannath. Finally a young maid was forced to do the job. To her utter surprise Jagannath removed his gold ring from his forefinger and gave it to her as *baksheesh.* Jagannath was genuinely pleased and he thanked her for bringing the wonderful news. The maid rushed back to flaunt the ring.

Girdhar longed to visit Radha and hold his daughter. But

nobody asked him to. His mother had assured him that both were fine. Men didn't go visiting their wives when they were confined. He would have to wait for forty days to catch a glimpse of his child.

Radha was shocked to see Girdhar, at the door of her dimly lit, ill-ventilated room.

"*Hai-Ram*!" She shrieked. "Why did you come here? What if someone sees you? They'll all say you're so shameless."

It took a few seconds for Girdhar's eyes to adjust to the dimness inside.

"Your mother has gone to the temple. And I have tipped the maid. She won't utter a word. I couldn't help it. I had to see you and her."

Girdhar picked up the small bundle of wrinkled skin. As he picked her up he felt like he had never felt before. It was happiness, fulfilment and peace, all at once. As he touched her cheeks, he could feel his hair bristle on his arm and his skin tingle.

"Radha, do you know, she looks like you?"

"No, she looks like *Maa*, everybody says so. She has her eyes and the very same nose."

Girdhar smiled. "How do I know? I have never seen your mother's face. She is always veiled. May be you look like your mother too."

"Radha", Girdhar continued, "you've put on a little weight, it's making you look sweeter."

Radha didn't reply. She kept winding the end of her sari on her finger.

"Aren't you happy to have her?"

"I don't know."

"Why?"

"She doesn't let me sleep. I have to keep feeding her the whole night. I wish I could leave her and go where I can sleep, undisturbed and where I can't hear her cry." Her large eyes had begun to fill and her thick eyelashes were heavy with tears.

"*Maa* gets me big *laddus* and milk at five in the morning. Tell me, can I eat sweets when all I want to do is sleep? So many times I just throw the *laddus* out of the window. I am not allowed to open the windows and let in fresh air. It's so suffocating here."

Radha buried her face in her palms and cried. The baby stirred a bit. Girdhar rocked her a little. He didn't know how to react to this sudden outburst of emotions. He hadn't expected this. Still he sympathised with Radha. Indeed it was stuffy and hot inside. This little girl had suffered a lot. The delivery had left her emotionally drained and irritable. At fourteen girls are supposed to play and here was his Radha, unable to handle a little live toy.

Somewhere Girdhar felt guilty. He was partly responsible for her plight. He lovingly glanced at his newborn daughter.

"No my child," he thought, "I won't put you in a situation like your mother. You won't be married so early."

Radha was still sobbing. Girdhar wanted to distract her. He thought of something to say. He debated with himself if he should tell her what was uppermost on his mind.

Radha had an independent and sharp mind. Girdhar knew that. He also knew she was capable of taking decisions herself and she would mature into an intelligent woman.

"Radha, I have decided to wear only *khadi* clothes in future."

Her face brightened with curiosity. "Why would you want to wear thick handspun cloth?" she asked, wiping the tears with the back of her hands.

"Gandhiji has appealed to us to wear only *khadi.*"

"Who's Gandhiji?"

"He's our leader. He's agitating against the British to get us freedom."

Before Radha could ask what freedom was, Girdhar explained.

"We have had enough of foreign rule. Why should others

rule us? We will have our own Rajah and we'll make rules which are favourable to us."

"If we wear *khadi,* will they go away?" Radha asked innocently.

"No, it is just a way to protest. It is to send a message that we will not accept anything that is British—not even their cloth."

Radha thought for a while and then said, "Do you know the brocade we use for our *ghagra,* the *gota* and the silk thread we use for our embroidery and even the needles we use are all 'Made in England'? The mirrors, glass and marble used to build our house is all from 'outside'. What will you do with it?"

Girdhar listened, but didn't say anything. His thoughts were elsewhere.

"Have you asked your father?"

"He doesn't approve much. He feels I shouldn't bother with politics. I should concentrate on business."

"If your father doesn't approve, don't do it." Radha advised. Girdhar didn't reply, only kept looking at Radha.

"Do you expect me to give up wearing English cloth?"

Radha tried to gauge Girdhar's mood.

"No, I don't."

Radha was relieved.

"You know, maa has just ordered two brocade *ghagras* for me. One is peacock blue and it has beautiful *zari* flowers and leaves running up its length. The other is pink with delicate *buti*. My cholis are embroidered with *salma, sitara.*" She paused for a moment, looked up at him with questioning eyes and continued cautiously, "the sequins too are made in England!"

Girdhar laughed. "You needn't worry Radha. I won't force you to wear *khadi.*" He got up to leave. "I'll come again," he said.

"No, don't," Radha shot back. Girdhar ignored it.

"By the way, I forgot to tell you. Father has bought acres

and acres of gardens next to our house. Our children will play there."

"Can't I play too?" Radha said instantly.

"Oh Radha, you are such a simpleton. Are you going to play? You are a mother now."

He saw the disappointment on her face. He didn't want to leave her that way.

"All right, we'll put swings on the Banyan and neem trees. You could go there and have fun. There are several jamun, guava and mango trees in the vast orchards..."

"I love climbing trees," she added hurriedly.

Radha spoke and then caught herself. Girdhar laughed simultaneously, nodding his head as if to say 'you're impossible'.

Radha too couldn't help laughing at herself.

For once Kesar maa forgot her Gopal. Day after day, from morning to night she was at Radha's side. She would hurriedly attend to Gopal to be with Radha. For the first time she felt close to her mother. Maa truly loved her and cared for her. Will she love her daughter as much? Radha often wondered. Right now she was more of a trouble. Radha had never felt any emotion towards her child.

"I don't think I can handle her, you keep her maa," she had once told Kesar maa, when the infant had cried all night. Exhausted owing to lack of sleep and frustrated because she was at a loss as to what to do, this was the only way she could think of to get rid of her newborn.

"No," Kesar maa replied firmly, "as you will feed her, bathe her, hold her close to you, you will develop a bond with her. You will love her like you have loved nobody, not even me."

She was called Krishna. She received undivided attention and love from her grandfather, who carried her wherever he went. Her grandmother took care of her so that Radha could relax a little. The battery of servants fussed over her. She went for long evening strolls with Bhima each evening. Jagannath had bought a 'Made in England' pram for her from Mumbai. Bhima converted it into a *baggi*. He attached it to the leather jacket of Moti, their brown and white dog. So, Krishna sat in the midst of soft, frilly satin cushions and surveyed her grandfather's orchards. She enjoyed these rides thoroughly. Jagannath was pleased to see Krishna in such a splendid *sawari*.

"We had a Queen in England and one right in our home," he had commented one day. He pampered her no end. Frocks and toys, fruits and dryfruits were all purchased from Mumbai; most often they were all 'Made in England.'

But Girdhar wore only *khadi*. The nation's call for young blood to join the freedom struggle appealed to him greatly. He started attending meetings held by the freedom fighters. Jagannath thought it was foolish to neglect a flourishing and expanding business. Land and properties required careful supervision to be economically viable. Instead of constantly showing his displeasure, he asked Girdhar to take on more responsibilities. He said he tired easily these days and felt a pain in his chest sometimes. The *Vaidji* dismissed it as *vayuvikar* and treated him accordingly.

He found happiness only in Krishna. He wanted her to be around him constantly. He found solace in her soft voice and cheerful disposition. Proving all predictions wrong, Krishna wasn't growing up into a spoilt, temperamental girl.

Jagannath was very proud of her and admitted she was the only weakness in his life.

The only person Krishna feared was Munimji whom she called Munim Dadaji. His big blood shot eyes scared her. Krishna didn't venture anywhere near Munimji. She avoided him like debtors avoided his recovery summons. Behind a large desk he worked endlessly, keeping accounts in long red account books. These books or *bahi-khata* were bound in red cotton cloth stitched with thick white thread. They were indispensable and vital for any business. Invariably, they consumed most of Munimji's working hours. He bent over them till his neck and back ached and his eyes went red with strain. On the right was a round brass inkpot with a lid and a brass box, which held sand. It was used to blot the ink stains. His desk held stamps, paper, pens and a box of small *churan* balls. The sweet sour *churan* balls with raisins were sucked after lunch as a digestive. Krishna loved them but was too scared to ask for them. Small change was kept in a copper bowl.

He hung his bright orange *pagdi* on a hook, on the wall when he was working.

Munimji was the head accountant and was responsible for most of the finances. Each month he sent Rs. 5 to Radha and her mother-in-law for personal expenses. The women awaited their pocket money. The five silver glistening coins with George V engraved on them brought smiles to their faces. They also received ten *tolas* of gold each year at Diwali.

Munimji had the authority to ask Girdhar to curb his expenses if he felt he was over-spending.

Each week Krishna received two copper *paisas*. She put them in her clay piggy bank or spent them in buying roasted *chana* and *murmura*. Krishna insisted on having pockets in all her frocks, so that she could fill them with various things. The roasted *chana* she bought, the almonds, cashews and raisins Radha gave her. Occasionally it would be shiny pebbles she found in the vast orchards, sometimes the unspent two copper coins she received from Munimji. Nobody had access to her treasure. She protected it from inquisitive prying servants, and even from her mother. Only Jagannaath knew what treasure her pockets held every day, whom she showed with great excitement and he in turn saw it with equal zeal. Her small secrets she trusted and shared only with him.

Munimji received a salary of Rs. 15 per month, with which he supported his family. He lunched with Jagannath every afternoon. At noon, both would proceed towards the kitchen.

As they climbed the stairs, Munimji would clear his throat or cough. This announced their arrival and the women pulled the veils over their faces. Absolute silence prevailed in the upper floors then. Women spoke in hushed tones and the crackle of the firewood became very apparent. The clang of the tongs as the cook roasted *rotis* on red-hot coal seemed louder then.

The women waited a little away from the men, alert if they asked for anything. Pusibai served them with quick efficient movements. Before starting the day's cooking the *maharaj* would demarcate the cooking area with a charcoal line. Nobody but a high-class Brahmin or Brahmini could touch the cooked food. The women ate after the men had left. Krishna always chattered while they ate.

'Thud,' the wooden stairs said as Krishna put her right foot carelessly on them. The bells of her anklets jingled. In her excitement, Krishna had forgotten to tread softly.

"Who is it?" Munimji's resonating voice echoed. His face was still buried in his account book but his eyes looked up and halted at Krishna. Red threads, running like rivers on a map, filled his eyes.

Krishna stood rooted. His eyes always did this to her.

"Where are you going?"

"Nanima's place."

"Why?"

"Mother asked me to..."

"Does your mother find it so difficult to look after her only child, that she keeps sending you away? Go back upstairs," Munimji said angrily.

Krishna mustered courage, and avoiding his eyes said, "Nanima has decorated her *puja* room with flowers today. Mother asked me to go for *darshan*. If you say no, I won't go." She turned a little to return.

"*Accha, accha* go, but not alone, take Bhima with you. And return soon." Munimji gave the permission to go.

As she crossed the wooden threshold, she saw Jagannath approaching. She ran and hugged him at the knees. She looked up, her large eyes glistening with tears. She looked into his eyes. So gentle and loving. So different from those fierce eyes she had just left behind. Krishna loved those crinkled eyes when he smiled. Her grandfather's eyes smiled along with his lips, she thought. She found comfort in their warmth now.

"What is it my child?" Jagannath had guessed that Krishna wanted to say something.

"Why does Munim dadaji scare me so much? You don't scare me."

"Because he cares for you *beta,*" Jagannath explained.

Krishna didn't believe him. If he cared he wouldn't scare her so much. He would have been gentle like her grandfather. And he wouldn't have those frightening eyes. But she didn't argue with her grandfather.

"You are going to Nanima's place aren't you?"

Krishna nodded to say yes.

"Tell me, how is your Nanima's Gopal faring? He must have put on weight, with all the *pedhas* and *rabdi* your grand mother makes for him. He was always so *gol-matol*. He's a real *chatora, nahi?*"

Jagannath could always make Krishna laugh.

She forgot those red eyes and laughed with her grandfather. "Nanima says she will teach me to make all that Gopal eats when I grow up."

"That's very nice, but you hurry up now, Nanima must be waiting for you. You should visit her every day, she's all alone you know."

Krishna ran away, Jagannath watched her little frame recede with Bhima at her side.

Why did this little thing enchant him, he thought, as he stepped inside his mansion. Poor girl! She was so terrified of munimji. Munimji shouldn't be so strict with this little bundle of joy. He saw munimji engrossed in his books. He smiled to himself. No, not even he as the master of the house could ask him to do that. He was as much her grandfather as he himself was.

"Nanima, Nanima," I have come, Krishna called out as she climbed the stairs as fast as her legs could carry her. Krishna loved to be with Kesar maa. She followed her around the house, asking question after question. She prayed with her and chanted hymns. She picked up a rosary and put her small hands in a *gomukhi*. She moved a bead forward and said, "*Shri Krishna Sharnam Mama*" like Kesar maa constantly chanted. Sometimes she lost patience.

"Nanima, enough now, I am hungry." She would sit before the almirah where Kesar maa kept the *prasad*. In the corner was a small bamboo basket, where Kesar maa kept small pieces of papers. She gave *prasad* to anyone who came visiting her. Nobody left the house without eating it on those small paper rectangles.

Krishna waited with the largest piece of paper she could find in the basket. A larger piece would accommodate more *prasad*.

"We get so much to eat because of Gopal. You should make more and more things for him."

Kesar maa watched Krishna demolish every peanut, every bit of sweet with great relish. She couldn't help remembering Radha as a child. Her anger, her jealousy towards Gopal. She had rejected Gopal, but Krishna had accepted him. It was because of him that she ate delicious sweets. Gopal filled her grandmother's empty days and hers with fun.

Krishna created small ripples in the quiet, peaceful life that Kesar maa led. She eagerly waited for her to come and hear her feet follow her everywhere. She got used to her endless chattering now. She told her stories of Lord Krishna and Radha, of Ram and Sita.

One day she told Krishna, "Your mother will bring you a brother now."

Without a moment's hesitation, she had said, "I want a sister, to play with."

Her wish was fulfilled.

Radha gave birth to a baby girl. This time all the servants wanted to break the news to Jagannath. Two of them bolted across to do so. Jagannath heard the news and turned to leave. He saw the two waiting in anticipation.

"Run along you two, do you expect me to celebrate the birth of a second daughter?"

Both had returned with crestfallen faces.

But Krishna had rejoiced. She touched the baby's soft fair cheeks to make sure she was real. She saw her red lips and asked her mother, "Has she eaten *paan*? Her lips are so red."

Radha saw Krishna so delirious with joy that she never regretted the birth of a second daughter. She was happy for Krishna's sake. If it were a son she would never be so happy. She tried to memorise within her heart the joyous face of Krishna. These moments were so rare. They had to be treasured. Kesar maa had been right. Krishna had given a new dimension to her life. She had taught her to love.

Jagannath named her Rukmini after Lord Krishna's beautiful and intelligent wife. Jamna wasn't too happy with a second granddaughter. Her endeavour to hide her feelings failed miserably. She rarely showed any warmth towards Rukmini, and it hurt Radha.

Nineteen-year-old Radha mellowed and matured into a responsible housewife and mother. She woke up at the crack of dawn, to supervise the household chores. Once in a while she did inquire when India would get its freedom.

"Very soon," Girdhar would say because freedom fever was at its peak. More and more people joined the struggle and were now demanding *poorna swaraj* or complete independence.

Radha sensed Girdhar's dilemma. He was keen to join the struggle in a more active way, but knew it would make his father unhappy.

"If I had a brother, I would go and live with Gandhiji," he often told Radha.

Radha was relieved.

"Thank God he doesn't have one," she thought. Girdhar was morally bound to live with his parents. *Pitru Rina, Matru Rina* had to be fulfilled first. Indebtedness towards the motherland came much later. The ancient scriptures said so. Sensible of the sage, who wrote *Yajurveda* for getting the priorities in the right order, Radha thought.

But in his own small way, Girdhar supported the freedom struggle. He stopped using and selling British goods. But he couldn't avoid dealing with the British officers who had to be entertained once in a while.

Krishna brought a message for Radha. "Baba has asked me to tell you, that we are having two English officers for tea."

"Tea? But I don't know how to make tea," Radha said

The household was in a hot debate. Each had a different recipe and each thought his was the correct one. Finally Girdhar procured the recipe from an acquaintance. But there was no teapot or cups and saucers in the house to serve the tea in. Girdhar hurried and arranged for a tea set from an old Parsee friend. It had a beautiful blue and gold border and the women promptly practised arranging it on a silver tray. But used clay vessels were not allowed in the kitchen. So a stove was lit on the terrace where the tea was finally prepared.

The Englishmen sat awkwardly. They appeared obviously uncomfortable sitting cross-legged on the thick *gaddi.* Girdhar apologised. "You see Indians eat on the floor, so our households do not have tables and chairs where we could serve the tea."

The Englishmen said that they understood. Girdhar asked Bhima to put the large bolsters behind them to rest their backs on. They rested their elbows on them and tried their best to look comfortable. Both the parties refrained from mentioning the freedom struggle. The conversation was strictly business.

The servant arrived balancing the jittery, clattering teapot and cups. He placed the hot *samosas* and syrupy *jalebis* before them. He served the snacks as Girdhar explained that *samosas* were spicy mashed potatoes stuffed in thin flour *rotis.* He explained in detail how the *roti* was rolled, filled with potatoes sealed and then fried.

The Englishmen were amused. The women, servants and Krishna had assembled behind the large teak almirah. They were all anxious to see how these *gore log* drank and even managed to enjoy the bitter *kalapani*. Turn by turn they peeped, hidden behind the almirah.

They giggled when the *gore log* found the *samosas* spicy and kept sticking their tongues out. Bhima quickly served water. One of the officers dug his teeth in the *jalebis* and the sugar syrup dripped on his white trousers. He sheepishly cleaned it with his handkerchief.

He looked at the crisp golden *jalebi* curiously and asked Girdhar, "How do you manage to fill sugar syrup in this thin wiry stuff? Do you inject it?" Girdhar couldn't help laughing, nor could anybody behind the almirah. The Englishmen ignored the joint laughter and giggles, which arose from behind the almirah.

Krishna had waited for the guests to leave. She followed Bhima with the tray. She poured the cold tea and milk in a cup, added the sugar and tasted it.

"It isn't so bad after all," she told Bhima who looked amusingly at her.

The tea episode appeared and reappeared in family conversations and discussions.

Krishna was six, and Rukmini two when they got a brother.

Everybody was relieved. A male heir would liberate them from worries in this world and their souls in the next.

Krishna anxiously waited for Rukmini to grow up so she could share her little joys and sorrows with her.

V

Solapur And Martial Law : 1930

7 May 1930

"Bharat Mata Ki Jai"
"Mahatma Gandhi Ki Jai"
"Vande Mataram"

The loud slogans drew the women out of their cool bedrooms. The dripping *khus* curtains and the round black fans kept their bedrooms scented and cool.

Radha stepped out hurriedly from her room, into a verandah and then the terrace. She withdrew her foot as the hot stone scalded it. She heard the crowd draw nearer. She ran for her wooden *khadau* and caught its knobs between her toes. Noisily she ran to look below. Her palms caught the railing. 'Oh!' She said somewhat irritated as she rubbed her palms that were scalded by the heavy iron railing.

Hundreds of men with white Gandhi *topees* and even a few women in white *khadi* saris, walked briskly in swarms, shouting, clenching their tight fists in the air, "*Nahi rakhna, nahi rakhna yeh jalim sarkar nahi rakhna.*"

Girdhar had told Radha that Gandhiji had been arrested and put into jail. There were widespread protests in the city. People were angry and were holding meetings everywhere. Something serious could happen he had warned.

She saw a *baggi* with a large portrait of Gandhiji on it. Over zealous people had garlanded it. As the carriage drew near her eyes opened wide. It was their carriage. A river of white pointy *topees* meandered its way in the streets of Solapur. Nobody had ever seen such fervour of patriotism before. People who stood by the sides of the roads, on the verandahs of their houses, on wooden planks of shops joined the mighty human river flooding the streets. Mesmerised and hypnotised, people joined the procession on impulse. Nobody knew where it was heading or what it would do. They just followed.

The carriage with the portrait was right below Radha now. She could see it shaky, and perched precariously. Suddenly the uncontrollable crowd pushed the carriage. The portrait fell shattering the glass. A minute of silence and then somebody stepped on the broken glass, picked the portrait and placed it on the carriage again. The river moved on. Radha, flushed and hot, wiped her sweaty face with her palm and wondered. This wasn't a good omen.

By evening there was great activity in the halls below.

The women peeped, and strained their ears to catch the conversation.

Girdhar and his father sat with a small crowd around them.

"This shouldn't have happened," someone lamented.

"It's our responsibility to maintain peace and our ignited feelings under control. It's easy to motivate and ignite violent emotions but the leader has then the responsibility to keep the mob under his control."

"There was no leader today to do that. They only spurred the crowd with fiery speeches and then let the situation get out of control." Jaju was agitated and angry. Jagannath tried to calm him down.

"That cannot be undone. What we have to aim at now is to get the situation under control before it worsens. The best way to do that is to let work begin normally. Let the shops open and factories operate. People will get busy in their daily routine and the violence will stop."

Jagannath had opposed the idea of public speeches and any sort of processions. Civil disobedience and Non-cooperation was Gandhiji's new experiment. It had evoked curiosity and a tremendous following throughout the nation. Like never before the freedom struggle of Gandhiji had penetrated the heart of

India, into the villages and the small towns. It was no longer concentrated in the urban areas and big cities, even the villages had responded overwhelmingly. Every Indian wanted to contribute for the movement to succeed. But Gandhiji had chosen the difficult path of non-violence. Not everybody could restrain the fire of patriotism burning within and simultaneously follow the path of non-violence. So people chose what was convenient for them or what they thought would be effective for the movement. Despite good intentions, sometimes there was lack of self-control and inability to control violence.

So, Jagannath had opposed the local leader's call for a public meeting. He had shown his displeasure when Girdhar had lent their carriage for the procession.

Now most of the local leaders saw sense in what he had said, some still did not.

They wanted to disrupt normal life to express their anger at the arrest of their leader.

The meeting had ended indecisively.

Radha was waiting impatiently in her bedroom for her husband's arrival. She was curious to know what was going on. Her regular informers, the male servants were unable to furnish her with satisfactory details.

The curtain of glass beads tinkled. Radha looked at the door expectantly.

The parrots on the bead curtain were beginning to settle down again. It was only a gush of wind.

This time the tinkle was louder.

Radha didn't wait for Girdhar to come inside.

"What's up? What's all this commotion downstairs?"

Girdhar looked surprised " Don't you know? The whole town knows about it by now."

Radha was offended.

Angrily she retorted, " How do you expect us to know sitting up here? Why didn't you take us along, it would save you the trouble of explaining?" she said sarcastically. "There were many women in the procession today."

"The procession was the cause of all the commotion today."

"As it left Tilak Chowk it went ahead to Civil Hospital then Sadar Bazaar, from there it proceeded to the Modi Bagh area. By the time it reached the Vishnu mill, there were thousands of people, all very excited."

" That's where we mainly get our cloth from. The Lakshmi, Vishnu mill, isn't it?

"Yes that is where trouble started."

" What happened?"

"Some workers continued working, a few came out to see and some joined the procession. Those who didn't stop work were pulled out and beaten mercilessly. The police was called to disperse the frenzied crowd."

"This is not what your Gandhiji wants you to do," Radha asked innocently.

" Of course not. But it's difficult to control the minds of thousands of people. Father had opposed the rally. But..."

" But you still went with it."

" How could I anticipate that a peaceful rally of Congressmen would turn violent?"

" But your father could. Why don't you go by your father's judgement? He is right most of the time. After all, experience counts."

Radha was always proud of her father-in-law.

Girdhar was quiet for a moment. Then asked her, "So when father says I shouldn't be wasting time in politics, I should listen to him?"

" Yes."

" Why?"

" Because your business suffers."

" Lakhs of men and women, who are selflessly struggling for our country's freedom, are they crazy? Young men don't think about their mothers and wives and their children's future when they go proudly to the gallows. They don't bother how their *choolahs* will burn after they are gone. Hundreds are languishing in jails and are sent away for life to *kalapani*."

"Do they think about their business, their career?"

"Haven't they all risen above themselves, above their own personal interests? If they did not, we will remain slaves forever. Let me tell you there are thousands of Marwaris too joining the freedom struggle. They have given effective leadership. Aren't you being selfish? Just give it a thought Radha, may be you'll get an answer."

Radha decided to remain silent for she knew Girdhar was in no mood to accept any argument rationally. Radha also saw the moral turmoil he was in, himself. His duty towards his country and his duty towards the family tore him apart.

She decided to sleep. But she couldn't. She was trying to find an answer.

The local leadership was divided.

Jaju, Jadhav and Rathi formed the older moderate group; Rajwade, Gulabchand and Khadkikar the second group; the third included Dr. Antroliker, Kurban Hussain, Kunjbihari, Shinde, Malappa Dhanshetty. This was the young energetic and do and die face of the leadership. Jagannath refrained from joining any particular group. He was sought by all when important decisions were to be taken.

The Rajwade group had distanced itself from Gandhiji's civil disobedience and non-cooperation ideology, thus becoming the target of criticism from the other two groups. Jagannath was neutral and so was the common link between all the leaders.

8 May 1930

After all the commotion of last night, the morning seemed very quiet.

Radha looked out into the streets. People had come out

but in lesser numbers. The chirping birds, the temple bells, the *mali* watering the orchards in front of the mansion, the sweeper sweeping the streets behind it. All seemed usual.

Then they heard gunshots at a distance. Everybody knew it meant trouble. Jagannath asked Girdhar to remain at home and walked out into the streets below. The street was quiet but some people had begun to gather.

Curious, what the noise was all about, wild guesses, false stories emerged.

But nobody knew the truth. Jagannath called for his carriage. He asked to go to his friend Dhanshetty's house. On reaching there, nervous relatives told him that he had gone to the Rupabhawani area.

"But why?"

Some people had informed him that hundreds of men had gathered there to uproot toddy trees. The crowd was getting violent and unruly. The collector and DSP had arrived with armed police. He had gone there.

"Rupabhawani," he directed his coachman. He heard more gunshots and as they drove on, they could hear loud sloganeering.

When he got there he was stunned. He saw hundreds of men go insane. Two police trucks and the collector's car were parked nearby.

The collector Night and DSP Playfair stood *gheraoed* by a large gathering. Frightened and knees wobbling, they were shielding their faces by burrowing them in their arms.

Bricks and stones were thrown at the police who stood ducked behind the trucks. Jagannath saw the bleeding body of a young man being carried and kept under a tree. He sensed the danger of more violence.

Suddenly he spotted Dhanshetty, snatching a thick *lathi* from somebody, waving it to disperse the shouting crowd he surged forward. People backed and made way for him, not knowing what he intended to do.

Dhanshetty reached the frightened Englishmen.

" Follow me," he shouted. " I'll take you out of here."

They followed, ducking behind him. Dhanshetty cleared a path for them. It took, great effort to push back an unruly and angry crowd and weave his way safely to the collector's car. Gasping and perspiring, he screamed.

"Go, just go away, otherwise you'll be killed," he told them.

Safe in the car, collector Night and DSP Playfair asked the driver to move. Humiliated and hurt, both could hardly conceal their anger. Their faces red and eyes spitting fire they didn't know what to do.

How could they face defeat from an unorganised, unruly and wretched crowd?

How could their saviour be a black native, armed with only a stick? How could they be so helpless?

As the car moved forward a stone came crashing on the windscreen.

" Fire," he told his police, reacting instantly.

"Fire," he repeated angrily and drove away.

What followed, left the crowd stunned. In one moment the tables had turned against them. Before they could react, men were falling around them, some injured, some dead.

Some fled, some stood rooted too scared to move, some fell on the ground face down, not knowing what to do. Suddenly the firing stopped. The trucks left. After a silence of a minute or too, there was chaos once again.

A small crowed surged towards Dhanshetty, their *shikar* was lost because of him. He was a traitor.

Jagannath anticipated the danger Dhanshetty was in. He thrust himself into the crowd pushing, pleading, making them see sense. But nobody listened. At last he got hold of Dhanshetty's wrist. Shielding him, he pulled him out and rushed towards his carriage. Slogans against him still continued. But then they let them go.

Inside the carriage, Dhanshetty was trembling. The tears

in his eyes shone, as he looked sadly at Jagannath.

"He betrayed us. I only meant to save him from the frenzied crowd. They would have lynched him otherwise."

He swallowed. "Don't you think it was my duty to do so?

"Aren't we all committed to non-violent agitation? At that moment I felt it could be disastrous if they killed Night and Playfair. It would have been a blunder on our part."

" I understand." Jagannath tried to comfort him.

"I saw it all. I understand your motive. Don't worry, people will understand when they return to their senses."

" My own people think I betrayed them. How could I do that? I couldn't even think of it." He shook his head to free his eyes from the tears.

"But how did all this begin?" asked Jagannath.

"A large crowd had gathered to fell toddy trees. Many had come just to watch. The collector and DSP came and gave orders to fire in the air. People began running in panic. Nine people were arrested. The crowd was asking for their release. The collector had refused, so the gathering started shouting and hurling stones at Night and Playfair. I only wanted to save them from the crowd but he ordered this brutal firing. So many must have been killed. Oh god! What will happen now?"

The carriage moved forward with two hapless passengers. They sat silently now, deep in thought. The creaking of the carriage made a small noise on the dusty road.

They didn't know that the crowd they had just left behind went into a frenzy when they saw nearly twenty-five people dead around them and several injured. A few helped the injured and took them to hospitals. The others gathered and together moved forward, screaming and bloodthirsty.

Someone shouted, "Get the police, get the police" and hundreds of hypnotised men echoed, "Get the police, get the police." The voice shouted again, "to Mangalwar Peth police station," and the voice echoed once again hundred times louder.

"Revenge! Revenge! Revenge!" The crowd screamed as

they reached the police station.

The human hurricane destroyed telephone poles, mangled wires and demolished anything that came its way.

When the police saw the crowd approaching, they closed the door and sought the back door. A few managed to run away. A few were caught and beaten.

The door fell easily under the immense weight of the crowd. People brought out furniture, files, cabinets, all that was inside into the open. Some had already fetched kerosene, which was poured on it and set afire. A young constable Chand was caught and beaten till he died.

People were fetching everything that could be burnt. Some one spotted a trembling policeman crouched, trying to hide under the table.

He was pulled out and as he was being beaten he pleaded, "Please let me go. I have small children."

He fell on someone's feet. A stick crushed a bone.

He moaned, "I am doing this job to feed myself, not because I am loyal to the British, please let me go."

Someone pulled him up and took him inside the police station. He was ordered to pull down photographs of George V and the Queen.

"Now kick it," a voice boomed.

Broken and battered, he couldn't move his leg. Someone kicked him. He lifted his other leg to kick and crumpled in a heap.

"Now urinate on it."

He could move no more.

"Urinate, you pig," someone hit him again.

Motionless, he passed urine.

Someone pushed the photographs under him.

They left him to find another prey.

They found one. Dada Jafar was hiding near the police station. He was instantly recognised and brought back to the police station.

The fifty-year-old asked for mercy. Hands folded, he fell

at their feet. "Please let me go, what have I done?"

Nobody heard his cries. He was beaten till somebody cried.

"Burn him."

"No o o!!" he screeched.

"Yes burn him."

Two caught his legs, two his hands and flung him into the burning furniture.

He crawled out, his clothes on fire.

He was pushed with sticks, back into the fire. The crowd watched his agony with no remorse.

They waited till his body stopped wriggling, till his legs stopped kicking, his arms stopped flaying, till his screams died altogether.

They watched this, unflinching and with great pleasure, as if their *atma,* their very souls had been taken away from them. They felt nothing, absolutely nothing.

They left the charred body of the unfortunate man, because a voice reminded them that there was more to do.

" To the court," it shouted and everybody turned towards the court.

The sun was shining bright and overhead. The *tandaav* was not over yet.

They invaded the court. The clerks, the guards, the lawyers were all taken by surprise. They ran out like frightened mice. The crowd laughed, teased and hurled abuse at them. Moments later the crazy people had the court to themselves. Someone occupied the judge's chair and sniggered menacingly.

An idea was born. The next moment someone stood in the witness box. Another enacted the role of a prosecutor, while the others quickly sat as spectators. The judge banged the hammer.

"The accused are guilty!" screeched the judge.

"I order them to burn the court as punishment. The verdict should be carried out immediately."

The verdict was received with loud clapping and shouting. The mock court echoed, "Burn the court! Burn the court!"

The senseless people ran out of the court, taking with them all they could lay their hands on.

They made a bonfire and danced around it.

Balls of cloth dipped in kerosene were flung into the court building. The wooden structure with hay roof caught fire instantaneously. The crowd cheered and clapped.

The sentence had been carried out! It was time to move forward.

As they spilled into the streets once again they caught policemen, beat them and replaced their caps with Gandhi *topees*. With nothing to stop them, they went hunting again.

It was past noon, the crowd was exhausted. Slowly the crowd thinned. But by now most of the police stations were empty. All the policemen had left their *chowkis* and escaped. The crowd had tied donkeys in the police station's premises. No one dared to remove them from there.

Fear gripped the city, as news of violence spread. Shops closed and people stayed inside. Only a few curious ones ventured out. Some children had come out on the streets to play. Otherwise the city of Solapur had come to a standstill.

The *khat-khat* of the *chaddar* looms, the sirens of cotton mills, the buzz of the bazaar, screaming hawkers, the drums following the dead and breast beating women possessed by *Devi* all fell silent. (Surprisingly no *Devi* would possess a woman till there were disturbances in the city). Nobody knew what would happen next.

The local leaders didn't know how to handle the situation. Any public meeting or a large gathering could lead to senseless mobs resorting to violence. All decided to stop their activities and wait till the situation was under control.

But this was not to be.

Like vultures on a decaying carcass two trucks descended on the paralysed city. City inspector Nepot, Sergeant Hall, Sergeant Solomon, Constable Muhammad Adam, Loco foreman Baxter, and a few railway police occupied one of the trucks. The second truck was full of armed police of the railway battalion, their Louis guns aimed from the windows. Two policemen lay flat on their stomachs on the roof of the truck, their guns in position. A few were armed with machine guns. Some walked the streets with scraping boots, bayonets flashing once in a while with a livid glint.

Suddenly, they were ordered to fire. For seven hours, from one o'clock to seven o'clock these trucks and men roamed the city, and fired at random. Men, women and children fell, dead or injured. A few were killed while sitting or standing in their balconies or on terraces of their homes. A few, who ran out to see what the noise was about, were shot on their doorsteps. Children were killed while playing outside their homes.

There had been no warning to stay indoors and so, a few who had dared to step out fell prey to this atrocity.

People were so frightened that they did not even dare to take the injured to hospitals. Relatives of the dead did not have adequate men to carry the corpses to the cremation ground. Some were carted while some had to wait for the next day.

9 May 1930

The president of the town, Manikchand Shah cried beside the body of his son Ratilal. The unfortunate boy had been standing on his terrace when he was shot and killed. His head and chest were shattered, staining the wall he was standing against a bright red.

His mother cried inconsolably. Silent mourners filled his house. Shocked people still could not believe what a handful of Englishmen had done yesterday.

In hushed voices they discussed and criticised.

There were scores of dead waiting to be cremated at the cremation ground.

A large crowd gathered to bid them a farewell, to sympathise with the relatives of the dead.

One woman died because she took her baby on the terrace for a breath of fresh air. She collapsed with her dead baby still clinging to her. Now they lay side by side on the funeral pyre for their final journey together.

A child died with his friend because he chose to play in front of his house. He saw men in trucks, guns aimed at him. Before he could comprehend what was happening, bullets penetrated his small chest. His friend's head was blown off. Men, who sat outside their closed shops, because there was nothing else to do, were killed, unawares.

People who had come to console did not have words, because the deaths were so unreasonable, so unjustified. The city was numb, and stupefied.

The cremation ground was dotted with pyres now ablaze. Jagannath stood with a group of people on one side. The heat from the pyre reddened their faces.

The futility of these deaths burnt their insides.

"What was the use of all the violence?" one said softly to the man next to him.

He nodded, "very true," he agreed sadly.

The man before them turned around and said, "It was barbaric. Eyewitnesses say that they saw the injured dying on the streets, crying for water and help, but nobody dared to go near them. They lay there for hours."

A few more people had joined them.

"Night was busy shifting English women and children to Pune in a special train. Why would he bother about our people dying like dogs on the streets?" Another caustic remark from a man who had just joined in. The voices were no longer hushed.

"Night ordered the firing to spread terror in the city. He wanted to divert the public's attention, while he reached the English women to safety."

"It was a revenge he took after what the mob did to the policemen in the morning."

"Why didn't he stop them from doing what they did? If

only two armed trucks had come that time the violent mob would have dispersed. He had ample time, till the court was burnt, till the *chowkis* were ransacked. But he sent the trucks in the afternoon, when everything was quiet, to kill harmless, innocent people. Why did he wait for so long?" An agitated voice spoke from the crowd.

Most of the people at the cremation ground had now congregated here. Jagannath was listening to what people had to say. He saw their anger and agitation.

"Don't you realise why Night waited for so long?" Jagannath asked.

"He wanted the mob to continue the rampage. He must have laughed at our stupidity. The mob thought they were taking revenge on Night. What did Night lose? The two policemen were our people. The police stations they destroyed were ours. The court they burnt was ours. When they are restored it will be from our money. The families of the dead will be compensated with our money. Who has paid for this violence? These men, women and children, burning here! Night was the least one affected. He was not even singed. And we think we took revenge! Let's not be mistaken. It's Night who has taken revenge, and left us gaping and stunned. He outsmarted us because we are irresponsible and stupid. We always allow the British to take advantage of us because they know we are foolish and emotional."

Jagannath had not intended to give a speech, at least not here. There was a deafening silence and people listened. Only the wood and bones crackled everywhere.

Jagannath looked at the grieving relatives, the swollen faces, the anguished red eyes, and the grief all over. The bones crackling in the leaping fires could have been his, or his son's, his wife's. The thought brought a lump in his throat. It was sheer luck that they were not standing in their balconies, or walking near their homes. A pity that Ratilal and several others weren't so lucky. The futility of violence became starker here at the cremation ground. Jagannath put his arm around a grieving father.

"This was no less than the Jallianwala Bagh massacre. Dyer went scott free. So will Night. Just wait and see. We can't do a thing against him." He shook his head in resignation. "We can't do a thing," he repeated sorrowfully.

The town was quiet. The police had left Solapur in terror and fled. The police stations were empty, no police officer daring to enter them. The Congress *swayam sewaks* manned the traffic and patrolled at night. The British officers had disappeared.

Once in a while the railway battalion patrolled the roads, but left as quickly as they came.

For three days the Congress ruled. The Congress tricolour showed up bravely at government offices, shops, homes and even at empty police stations. Courage and defiance was returning quietly but slowly.

11 May 1930

Jagannath had just finished dinner, when there was frantic knocking at the heavy, wooden door. Somebody was banging the locking chains against it. There was an urgency, which both Girdhar and his father sensed. Girdhar didn't wait for Bhima to arrive. He ran to the door.

"Who is it?" He called.

"Open up, it's important."

Girdhar recognised the voice of Vishwanath Desai, a dedicated Congress worker and a friend of Jagannath.

He let him in. Vishwanath hastily bolted towards Jagannath, without even greeting Girdhar at the door. Girdhar followed him.

"You must flee Solapur, today, now," he caught Jagannath's arm in a tight sweaty grip.

"Why?" They asked in unison.

"The British," he gasped, "they are arresting anyone who

they think is even remotely related with the mob. We have this information from a reliable source."

"But I wasn't in the mob."

"Your were seen with Dhanshetty. Night saw you."

"This is atrocious! Jagannath was angry. Dhanshetty saved Night and DSP Playfair from the frenzied mob that day. He would have been killed otherwise. Everybody knows it."

"Does the truth matter any more?

There is a strong rumour that Night wants Martial law in Solapur. Then he'll crack down on anyone he pleases; there will be no stopping him. He won't need any warrants or charges to frame anybody. We are all hiding till the matter cools down a bit."

"So we all run away like cowards? When we know we haven't done anything wrong?"

Girdhar interrupted them now.

"Baba, it's not being a coward when you know you will never get a fair trial. What's the use of getting arrested? You will never get a chance to prove anything. It would be sensible to hide till matters are quieter."

"We are leaving within an hour. We will all assemble at my house. But be discreet. Don't carry luggage. There is strict patrolling in every corner of the town. We will leave one by one, not together. Think of a valid reason for being out at night in case you are asked. I still have to contact a few people."

Vishwanath prepared to leave.

"Where will you go?" Girdhar asked anxiously.

"That we will not disclose."

"How do we know that you are safe?"

"We will let you know as soon as we can." Vishwanath left.

There was a hot debate in the house afterwards. But Girdhar remained adamant. He hid a bundle of notes in his father's vest pockets and prepared his father to leave. Wearing two *kurtas* under his long coat and a spare *dhoti* stuffed in his coat pocket, Jagannath disappeared into the shadows of the silent night. A half moon hung in the eastern sky, the sole witness of the night.

A tense Girdhar wondered whether he had taken the right decision to send his father away. He could only pray and wait.

12 May 1930

The town's administration was handed over to the army. Lieutenant General C.P. Page was the commanding officer. More than 500 British soldiers were called in and by 8 pm in the evening, "Martial Law" was proclaimed.

13 May 1930

There was no news from Jagannath. Girdhar was worried. He was in discussion with a few Congress workers when a truck with white soldiers screeched to a halt before their house. The group fell silent. A few charged in towards the group of men sitting, trampling the white mattress with their boots. One of them shouted.

" Who is Jagannath here?"

" My father." Girdhar tried his best to remain calm. His palms were already clammy. He kept sitting.

" Where is he?"

" He is away on a business trip."

"When will be return?"

"Can't say."

Girdhar's calm and poise infuriated the soldier.

"Get up you!" He barked. "What's that mark on your forehead?" The soldier pointed his finger towards the vermilion fork on his head.

" It's a *Tilak.*"

He pointed his butt towards a Maharashtrian worker who had a round red vermilion mark on his forehead.

"And what's that?"

"*Gandh.*"

"Bastards, Gandhi -Tilak ke aadmi hain!"

Girdhar and his men laughed at the joke created inadvertently, annoying them further.

"All of you get into the truck." Face red with fury, a few more soldiers had begun to goad them out of the house.

As the lorry moved, the soldiers snatched the Gandhi topees from their heads and trampled them with their boots.

"This is what has created all the trouble." He declared.

Someone snatched the gold watch from Girdhar's wrist; another lost his chain, someone his ring.

One soldier lit a few cigarettes and passed them to other soldiers. Sniggering, they burnt their faces, necks and arms. That's for laughing at us, you bastards."

"*Vande Mataram*!" The brave group kept chanting till they reached the police station. The cigarette burns had erupted into blisters and dotted their bodies.

They were questioned for hours, tortured and then finally released.

This group had been fortunate, because hundreds had been tortured and detained in jail. False cases were framed against them with no opportunity to say anything in defence.

Girdhar met his father's friend Dhanshetty and asked him to leave the town and go into hiding. He could continue the struggle when the present crisis subsided. He was in danger. Dhanshetty refused. Girdhar's efforts failed to convince him. He would face it, come what may.

The very next day on 14 May he was arrested, tortured and put into jail with many others. When Girdhar went to meet Malappa Dhanshetty, he could hardly walk and stand.

Burn marks dotted his whole body. Blood had congealed in thick patches on the front of his *kurta*. He had been brutally tortured.

"Hey Ram!" was all Girdhar could manage to say as he saw him wobble towards him. It could have been his father;

Girdhar shuddered at the thought.

"Was it worth it?" asked Girdhar. He couldn't bear to look at the battered body before him. But he forced himself to.

Clutching the bars between them, he continued, "You won't even get a fair trial, nobody will testify in your favour. Anyone who has come forward till now has been terrorised. They have withdrawn or changed their testimonies."

Dhanshetty appeared to be in great pain. He buckled and sat down. He raised his bloody head.

"Any news from Jagannath?"

Girdhar shook his head in denial.

" No, but a *Jhanda satyagrahi* from Nasik has informed us not to worry. He did not disclose anything further."

Girdhar swallowed.

"You could have gone too...look what they have done to you."

Two men came and quickly carried Dhanshetty away. He moaned in pain.

Girdhar returned distraught and head spinning.

"Aren't you relieved that your father was spared?" Radha questioned.

"I don't know. After seeing Dhanshettyji today, I think if father had been here he would have testified in his favour. He had said that he had saved Night and was not responsible for inciting the crowd. He had nothing to do with the police burning. He was with father at that time."

"Doesn't Night know that?"

" He knows. But perhaps the court would have listened."

"No, father would have been in jail, battered and broken. You know Night would never have let a crucial witness go free."

" I understand all that, but when I saw him, I felt guilty. Father is going to feel the same way, I know that." Girdhar looked pained and in doubt.

Radha wasn't.

"There is no need to feel guilty when you know father would not have been able to help him in any way. I am relieved that he is safe."

"I wish I could too, Radha," Girdhar said softly. "I wish I could think as clearly as you."

There was no news from Jagannath or his whereabouts. The family waited anxiously.

13 May to 14 May, Solapur

Under the Martial law, the white soldiers looted, terrorised, stole, robbed, ransacked, raped and revenged. People watched with stunned silence.

There was nobody to save them from the disaster befalling them. Hundreds were put into jail without any explanation.

Nobody knew when the anarchy and misrule would stop.

The military court sentenced hundreds of jailed men to imprisonment, fines, lashes or all. Girdhar was fined Rs. 500 for lending his carriage for the procession. He was constantly asked about his father's whereabouts.

29 May 1930

The collector's office was packed to capacity. The courts were still not repaired and functional, so Malappa Dhanshetty and the three other main accused in the police burning episode were to be tried here by a sessions court.

Girdhar had come early and occupied the first bench. City Inspector Nepot was the first witness to testify. He avoided looking at Dhanshetty throughout his testimony.

He said that Malappa Dhanshetty was the "backbone" of the rioting at Rupa Bhawani. He was responsible for inciting the crowd by his fiery speeches and the collective attack on him.

Girdhar saw Dhanshetty frustrated and angry. He shuffled

restlessly and was in apparent pain. He had requested Nepot and Night to release a few people who were arrested. Malappa Dhanshetty denied the charge. The court cross-examined him. "Were you present in the mob when the innocent policemen were brutally murdered?"

Dhanshetty -"No, I was not present."

Court - "And when they attacked the police station?"

Dhanshetty -"No, I was not present there either."

Court - " Did you drag the policemen out of the station?"

Dhanshetty -"No."

Court -"Did you murder them?"

Dhanshetty -"No."

Court - "Did you burn them?"

Dhanshetty -"No."

Court - "Do you want to say something in your defence?"

Dhanshetty -"Yes, I was acquitted from all the cases against myself in the Hindu-Muslim riot some months ago. The police had an eye on me ever since. The whole case is a farce. I have a few witnesses, but no one is willing to testify because they are afraid of the Martial law. I have been framed in a false case."

Girdhar was impressed with the confidence he spoke. Dhanshetty continued in his loud booming voice.

"We realise the outcome of this case. The police have collected false evidence against us but the court must know the truth. I was present in the morning when the mob was turning violent against Mr Night and DSP Nepot. I saved them from the mob by using my only weapon, a *lathi*, otherwise they would have been dead that day. We are followers of Mahatma Gandhi. He has never encouraged violence and revenge. In fact he has deterred us from following a path of violence. His teachings inspired me to save Night and Nepot that day. The court should present them with a Bible and ask them the truth. Ask them who saved them that day. I cannot understand why they are lying. Why they should implicate the very person who saved them is something I cannot comprehend. What sort of revenge is this?"

Dhanshetty paused, then defiantly looked at the judge with his big, black eyes.

"Yes, I was present that day. But it is only because I was present that day that those two are alive." The court fell silent. Dhanshetty continued.

"The court should seriously consider the fact that if I could save two white officers from being murdered, would I incite others to kill a petty Indian policeman, would I butcher my own countryman? After I saved them, the crowd turned against me, calling me a traitor. I had denied them their prey, and the bloodthirsty crowd would have me instead. A friend saved me and took me away, So, I can say on oath that I was not present thereafter. The crowd moved on but I was not with them."

Court-"Who took you away? Why doesn't he testify for you?"

Dhanshetty looked at Girdhar but he gave no answer.

Court-"Who saved you? Why don't you reveal his name?"

Dhanshetty-"Doesn't the court know?"

The court did not note a single word of what Malappa Dhanshetty had spoken in his defence. It noted only the false evidence against him. Three other accused were also tried that day.

They were:

(1) Shrikishan Sarda, a Marwari businessman, born and raised in a prosperous family. He had only recently joined the freedom struggle.

(2) Jagannath Shinde, a popular Hindu leader amongst the young freedom fighters. Known for his fearlessness and pro-Hindu leanings.

(3) A. Kurban Hussain, a fearless and dedicated man of twenty, striving for Hindu Muslim unity. He projected the image

of a true nationalist and a liberal Muslim.

All three denied having anything to do with the murders.

All requested the court to "see" that they had been implicated in a false case because of their political leanings.

6 June 1930

The session's Judge Mr. Wadia, awarded death sentence to all four for the 'hideous' crime they had committed.

"All four suspects had attacked unarmed and vulnerable policemen on duty. I cannot give a lesser sentence," he had announced.

On hearing the death sentence all four had shouted "*Vande Mataram*," "Mahatma Gandhi ki Jai."

Within eight days, their fates were sealed.

Martial law was lifted on 30 June 1930 after 49 days of its implementation.

The next day a notice was issued. The national symbol could not be displayed, no public meetings could be held, no processions could be taken out in the vicinity of Solapur. Challengers were promptly arrested and harassed. Fear still abided in the hearts of the people.

The accused appealed in the High court.

Girdhar attended the proceedings again occupying the first bench. Eyes fixed on Advocate Bhulabhai Desai as he appealed for all the four accused. For three days Desai struggled to convince the Chief Justice Boment and Justice Madgaonkar. The verdict given by both the Judges differed. Boment upheld the previous sentence, saying he believed Playfair when he said he witnessed the murder of the two policemen but Madgaonkar differed. He found only Dhanshetty guilty. The rest he acquitted, giving them the benefit of the doubt.

The three had to be tried again. On 1 August 1930 Chief Justice Baker found all three guilty, and so all four were to be hanged. If there was any hope for them, it ended with this sentence.

There was loud protest against the sentence. The trial had attracted the attention of the common man as well as the elite and the educated. Barriers of caste, creed and occupation crumbled as they took to the streets of Maharashtra and other states. Three lakh signatures were collected by elite women of Mumbai and sent to the Viceroy to spare the four.

Editors screamed from their columns at the unfair trial and injustice done to the freedom fighters.

People spoke fearlessly against the verdict at public meetings held to condemn the trial.

Letters were sent to England, but all efforts failed. The British would never miss the opportunity to teach the insolent and defiant Indians a lesson. By one single verdict they would spurn thousands and lakhs of Indians who were begging for the four lives. They had got the nation to their knees. It was tragic and ironic that they would not be saved from the noose because they had attracted a large section of public opinion in their favour. The convicted realised that the British would never reverse the verdict and let the Indians triumph.

Girdhar stooped over his desk dipping his pen in the black inkpot as he wrote on a white sheet of paper. Something cast a shadow on the paper.

Girdhar looked up. A lean, bearded man dressed in a dirty white *dhoti* and *kurta* looked down at him. His Gandhi *topee*, though dusty and brown, sat proudly on his head.

"Yes?" Girdhar asked. The man smiled.

The smile jerked Girdhar up in an instant.

"Baba! Baba! Baba!" was all he could manage to say. As reality sank in, Girdhar held his father's arm and hurriedly led him into the room inside. When alone, he said, "Baba, it's so nice to see you back safe. But it's not yet safe for you here. The police still come and ask for you. They have questioned me repeatedly. You should not be seen here for a while."

"Till when?" Baba asked. Girdhar swallowed.

"Till after the hanging." Tears filled his eyes.

"I have been following the case," his father said. He noticed the black, round, burn marks on Girdhar's face and arms but said nothing.

"Where were you?"

"Never in one place. But I have now come from Goa."

"Baba," Girdhar hugged his father.

"You must go back, right away, before someone recognises you."

" I'll go away but only after I have met Malappa. I must see him before he leaves us."

Girdhar saw how sadness had spread on his father's face. It had become thin and lined. He had lost so much weight that this *kurta* hung loosely on his shoulders.

"Baba you'll be taking a great risk. They'll arrest you. God knows what they will do with you. They still insist that they saw you with Dhanshetty that day. They will embroil you in a false case as was done with so many other people."

"No Girdhar, I have to see him. At whatever cost."

Girdhar realised his father wouldn't relent. He would have to find a way.

The household tearfully met Jagannath in a dim room upstairs. He was fed but Girdhar asked him not to change and wash. He had less chances of being recognised this way. Girdhar and Jagannath arrived at the prison in a closed *baggi* with Malappa's elder brother, Shankarappa.

Shankarappa met his brother frequently, so no questions were asked. Tears flowed as the two friends met. They embraced and smiled, trying hard to hide the sorrow within.

Malappa noticed how thin Jagannath had become. His dirty clothes and unkempt beard had completely changed his regal personality.

He grieved at what had happened to his friend.

"This is the price you had to pay for saving my life that

day," Malappa held Jagannath's hand in his as he spoke. His voice broke as he continued, "but no one can save us now, it's all over, Jagannath."

"Malappa, in fact I have come to ask for forgiveness. I will live with the guilt for not appearing to testify for you. I was witness to that day's happenings."

"Don't live with that guilt, my friend. Your testimony would make no difference to my sentence. You would have been here with me, in jail. Playfair and Night testified against me. Imagine, those very people whom I saved from the mad crowd that day. Do you think they would have considered your testimony when they were firmly determined to hang us? They didn't even write down anything said in our favour. Our fates were decided on the very day of our arrest. The trial was a sloppy farce. I am indeed relieved that your life is spared."

There was complete silence. Jagannath did not want to sound apologetic. The last thing he would do right now was to erode and weaken his friend's pride and fearlessness.

Shankarappa was too choked to speak. Girdhar thought it would be sensible to remain silent at this juncture.

Just then Jagannath Shinde was let in. Smiling, he greeted everyone.

"We share the same name sir," he addressed Jagannath, "and Malappaji keeps talking about you."

Jagannath managed to smile.

Shankarappa was trying hard not to break down. Finally he gathered courage to speak.

"Mallappa, all efforts to save you failed. Now there is only one course we can take," he spoke cautiously.

"Which course Dada?" asked Malappa.

"Seek clemency!"

Shankarappa felt his feet weak beneath him, he wanted to finish what was on his mind nevertheless.

"We'll send your signed letters seeking mercy to the Queen and the Viceroy. Malappa, don't refuse please," he implored.

Everyone was stunned into silence.

"You are such a simpleton, Dada, or are you fooling yourself into believing that our four signatures will change our fates?"

"People want you to live," Shankarappa said simply.

"But the government wants us to die," Shinde interrupted.

"We are grateful and fortunate that we have the sympathy of thirty three crore people. Let us die with that treasure."

Malappa had barely finished when Shinde interjected.

"Apart from this Dada, bliss in death and death in bliss are both so rare to achieve by ordinary mortals like us. By the grace of some divine benevolence, we can achieve both in our short lives. Don't deprive us of this golden opportunity."

Shankarappa, Jagannath and Girdhar stood quietly, too drowned in grief to answer. Tears flowed unchecked. To stop them was impossible now.

Malappa looked at his brother and said, "Dada, what would you prefer? That our future generations point at us and say he lives because he is afraid of death. He begged for his life and put his country to shame. Or would you prefer that they erect our statues with pride and remember us as fearless, proud, freedom fighters who died for their country? Let us be remembered as self-respecting men who died with dignity."

"Now that our death is certain, allow us to be a little selfish and wish such a glorious death," Shinde said, his smile lighting up his eyes now.

How could Shinde still manage to laugh and be happy, Girdhar wondered.

Shankarappa was discouraged. Nothing moved them, nothing made them see sense. He had one last arrow in his quiver.

He decided to use it.

"Malappa, Jagannath not for anybody, do it for your young children."

"Please Dada don't weaken us by using this strategy. When God gives life, He provides for it. He will protect them. I am sure."

The visitors left the prison feeling helpless and sad. As Jagannath left his friend Malappa, both knew this was the last time they would be seeing each other.

Malappa saw Jagannath's receding figure. He waited for him to turn one last time. Just before the door, Jagannath turned. There were no words, no gestures.

Their eyes met and bid each other farewell.

Malappa Dhanshetty, Shinde, Husain and Sarda here hanged on 12 January 1931, at Yerawada Jail, Poona.

Jagannath could only return eight months later.

The four martyrs were immortalised when their statues were erected in the heart of the city on the 1 August 1953.

The place is known as 'Hutatma Chowk'.

Nobody in Solapur would forget their sacrifice.

VI

Krishna-Rukmini-Shree : 1939

"Krishna, Rukmini; you both won't go to *shala* today. I want you to help me make a *Gangaur*. Krishna, you stitch the clothes and Rukmini will make *mogra* and thread garlands for the *puja*. I'll be very busy in the kitchen," Radha announced to her daughters that day.

Marathi words had stealthily crept into Marwari vocabulary. School was referred to as *shala* and apple was called *safarchand*. Hundreds of Marathi words replaced their Marwari synonyms and ungrudgingly remained there forever.

Marwari children learnt their tables in Marathi, sang Marathi songs and read Marathi literature. Girls gave up the cumbersome *ghagras* for the more manageable *parkar-polka*. *Parkars* were long, slightly pleated skirts with short blouses. Slowly Marathi culture blended into the Marwari lifestyle like Kesar maa's *makhan mishri*. The castor sugar at first retained its hard identity, but gradually melted to become one with the white butter.

Eight-year-old Rukmini looked at her sister to see her reaction. There was none. "Maa, we cannot miss school whenever you wish. Our 'Master' (teacher) gets angry with us, moreover he is starting a new lesson today, and I won't miss it. Jiji will go too," Rukmini protested.

"Then you go to school without your tiffin," Radha said firmly.

Krishna sensed her mother's anger mounting, she found a safe way out.

"Rukmini, you go, I'll stay to help mother."

Rukmini wasn't convinced with her decision.

"You shouldn't miss school just for nothing."

But Krishna insisted. Rukmini went to school without her tiffin. She didn't say a word in protest. Too proud to say anything, she went to school. The whole morning Krishna worried about Rukmini. "Poor girl, she must be hungry," her thoughts were constantly with her sister as she tottered after her mother, doing just as she was instructed.

Rukmini wasn't hungry. She had bought cucumbers and guavas on her way to school. She sprinkled salt and red pepper on them before she ate them during the lunch break.

"Poor Jiji, she had to miss school," she regretted.

Munimji grew very fond of Rukmini. As a routine she sat next to him every afternoon with a black slate. He gave her sums to solve. She added, subtracted, divided and multiplied. When she finished solving them, she pushed the slate towards him often placing it on his account books, stopping his work. If he was displeased, he rarely showed it, and gave her a fresh set of sums. His red eyes and his powerful personality didn't intimidate her. Krishna wondered how she could sit for hours with Munimji. Rukmini received a paisa as reward if all her sums were correct. She hid this treasure beneath her clothes, in the cupboard. It came in handy to buy cucumbers if mother sent her without tiffin or to bribe someone to get her job done.

While Rukmini roamed with her brother, Krishna learnt to sew and embroider. In general she was being trained to be a 'good girl'. She rarely annoyed her mother, while Rukmini invited her mother's wrath every other day. Radha felt helpless whenever she had to deal with Rukmini. Sometimes she did manage to rein her physically but she could never rein her exuberance, independent thinking and fearlessness. It irritated Radha when Rukmini did exactly what she thought was right; not what she was told.

Radha often complained to Girdhar "I am worried about Rukmini. Do you realise what will happen to a girl with her disposition? She will never adapt herself to any family. She's headstrong and obstinate, always wants her way. She doesn't..."

"She never argues or talks arrogantly. She respects her elders and her teachers are extremely pleased with her. Don't compare her with Krishna. This girl is different and you cannot help that. Her interests are different, just let her be."

Girdhar defended his daughter.

"You think even her in-laws will spoil her like you do? They'll say, her mother hasn't taught her a thing. Nobody is going to point a finger at you; it's me they are going to blame. Daughters are our responsibilities. No wonder you look the other way ignoring all her arrogance."

Radha looked worried. Her eyebrows arched inwards, eyes crinkling. She endeavoured to make her husband see sense. It seemed a futile attempt. It made her more agitated. Girdhar sensed it. To appease her, he said, "Radha, she's just a child, why don't you..."

Radha didn't let him complete his sentence. "Oh really? I was married to you at that age," she observed drily.

But Girdhar didn't mind it. He always let Radha score on this argument. Like always, he softened.

"Don't you think you were robbed of your childhood? Do you realise Rukmini is so much like you? There is a lot of you in her. The streak of vivacity and vitality you possessed is so apparent in her. Only you accepted to be tied down. Don't try to bundle up a sunbeam. Let it shine brightly." His eyes implored.

Tears welled up in Radha's eyes. It was true, she saw so much of herself in Rukmini but had refused to accept the fact. The pool in her eyes brimmed over into shiny streams on her smooth fair cheeks. They hesitated a little at the roundness of her cheeks and then gathering momentum fell rapidly down the slopes of her face onto her arms. Girdhar held her face in his palms and wiped the tears with his thumbs.

Rukmini located Shree near the fountain. Five big watermelons sank in its waters like some wreckage. Rukmini eyed them but knew she would only get to eat them when they were declared cooled by one of the elders. Till then she would have to wait. Shree was counting marbles. He had won an enormous amount today. His pockets swelled with them. Shree kept slapping his pockets to hear the music they made. He loved to hear his victory.

"Wah! What a win!" Rukmini tried to gain his attention. He continued counting.

"Shree, will you teach me to swim?"

"What?" He presumed he had heard her wrong.

Rukmini repeated it, stressing each word.

"Have you gone crazy? If Maa hears of it, you won't be scolded this time, but spanked."

"I'll handle all that, just take me along this afternoon."

"No, I won't."

"But why?"

"Because I don't know how to swim myself. Bhima ties a tin canister on my back and lowers me into the well with a rope around my waist." Rukmini couldn't help laughing at this.

"Like he takes our dog Moti for a walk?" Rukmini regretted teasing him as soon as she had said it. She realised it was a wrong move at a very crucial moment. She shouldn't have teased him now. Not when she was negotiating a deal. Shree made a face.

"I won't take you all the more. I'll tell Maa. Just see."

Rukmini saw her plan shattering. She had to save it, and act fast. She told herself, "one must be careful of what to say and when. It can spoil many things."

"Munimji gave me a paisa yesterday and I have four more annas with me. I'll give it to you if you take me along."

It was a princely sum. Four annas meant hundreds of marbles, kites and candies. An opportunity to show off before his friends. It was an irresistible offer.

"All right, but if maa comes to know, I'll take no responsibility," said Shree, sounding very important. It was rare that he got to boss over his sister. Usually it was she who decided what to play, where to go and what not to do. Rukmini nodded happily at the success of her deal. She was already thinking.

It was four o'clock. The summer afternoons were always lazy and sleepy. Radha retreated into the quiet of her teak wooded, Belgian glassed bedroom. She had to stand on her toes to get on the high, engraved wooden bed. It was a time she looked forward to. It gave her a welcome break between the end of the morning chores and the beginning of the evening tasks. The children used this time to do all those things they were otherwise restricted to do. They awaited it as much their mother did. She, to take a break from the activities, and they to break into activities. Girdhar was on a business trip to Mumbai.

Krishna had already been taken into confidence. She was somewhat reluctant at first but relented for her sister's sake. She promised to handle the situation in her absence.

Danger lurked only with Munimji. He had his lunch early and by now would be alert after his afternoon nap.

Shree and Rukmini craned their torsos and necks through the railings of the staircase. On the wall hung his bright orange *pugree* like the stuffed head of a tiger with its tongue hanging out. Rukmini saw it and jerked herself out of the railings. His *pugree* had done the job his eyes usually did. Like a faithful employee.

She anticipated that the first step on the staircase would evoke a response from him of a booming "who is it?." But only if he heard the tinkle of her anklet bells. Rukmini quickly removed her silver anklets and hid them in a blue glass flowerpot near the staircase. She had unshackled herself. She held Shree's hand. Both drummed down the stairs in unison, as if only Shree was thumping down the stairs. Munimji hadn't bothered to look up because he hadn't heard the anklets.

"Is that you Shree?"

Two thumping hearts were ready to burst out. Shree was too scared to speak. Rukmini pinched him.

"Yes, Munimji." Shree blurted.

"Where are you going?"

"To the farm, with Bhima"

"Come back before dark. Be careful in the water," Munimji warned them.

"Yes, Munim dadaji."

Both ran out noiselessly, breathing only when they crossed the high wooden threshold. It was the first taste of freedom and Rukmini relished it.

Bhima lowered her in the well with a rope around her waist. He walked round and round on the rim of the well while Rukmini learnt to swim. Shree clapped his hands and shouted into the well, his voice echoing, "Moti, Moti."

Shree shared the joy with his sister, when on the seventh day she climbed down the steps without the rope.

An excited Rukmini rushed to Krishna to break the news. After all for seven days she had made excuses for her sister. She had shielded her whenever mother enquired about her.

She became a heroine at school. The girls *ooohhhed* and *aaahhhed* disbelievingly. Some looked at her with awe, some with admiration, some declared she was too cheeky for their liking. Rukmini liked to see the shock on their faces. Smugly she declared she would come to school on a bicycle on the fifteenth day from now. Girls didn't cycle to school. They came in horse driven *baggis*, often accompanied by escorts.

She threw the challenge at herself. She would need Shree's help again. She had to learn cycling before the school closed for the summer holidays. She lured her brother with her share of homemade mango ice cream.

After the schools closed, when the dry heat baked the earth and humans, the children longed for the yearly ice-cream ritual.

Radha thickened the milk and added sugar, mangopulp, saffron and cardamom. This went into the drum of the wooden pail. Enthusiastic children crushed the ice. The ice went in with the salt stones between the drum and the pail. Then began the wait that seemed endless. Turn by turn the children turned the handle lifting the lid impatiently to see if the milk was freezing properly. They never left the site for a moment. After more than two hours the hovering children settled down with large silver bowls. Radha gave them huge dollops of the delicious golden stuff, which enticed them each year into doing this frantic dance around a measly wooden pail. Radha allowed the three children to invite a friend each to this ice-cream eating ritual. They all sat in a circle licking and chattering. Each ate it as slowly as they possibly could, hoping to finish last.

This year, Rukmini decided to forego her share of ice cream because she wanted to put before Shree an offer he couldn't refuse. She debated with herself whether it would be wise to trade her delicious, once-in-a-year ice-cream with Shree to learn cycling. She concluded, learning to ride a bicycle was more important. Shree had accepted as she had anticipated.

Learning to cycle had been easier than the swimming stint. She just had to go to the vast orchards with Shree. On the last day of school, a euphoric Rukmini cycled to school, with the horse driven *baggi* following her. Once again she stole a sunbeam for herself.

That summer Shree got double his share of ice-cream, while Krishna shared hers with Rukmini. Radha had heard that Rukmini was riding bicycles with Shree. She showed her displeasure by not saying a word about it. Her daughter wouldn't stop doing it anyway. When would she learn to cook and embroider, she wondered.

A missionary school had opened its doors for the local children. Girdhar decided Shree should be removed from the Marathi medium school and enrolled into this "English medium school."

He felt that knowledge of English would be advantageous while dealing with the British businessmen. He had faced this difficulty himself.

When he told Radha about his decision she was furious. She decided to confront him.

"Does it mean that you believe we are not getting freedom?"

"No, it doesn't mean that" Girdhar replied thoughtfully.

"Then why does Shree need to learn English?"

"Because even if the *'Angrez'* leave this country, English is going to be used for years to come. It will help him in business," Girdhar explained folding and unfolding his boat shaped, starched white *khadi topee*.

"He could learn English from a private tutor at home. He need not go to a school where they don't say our prayers, don't believe in our God, don't celebrate our festivals. I heard they don't teach how great a warrior Shivaji was, or Prithviraj Chauhan was, but make the children learn how great their Raja is. Why should we teach our children all this? I would like my son to grow up with the teachings of Tulsidasji and Guru Ramdas." Radha's voice had turned shrill, her agitation quite apparent. But Girdhar seemed quite unmoved and unperturbed.

His calmness angered her all the more. She realised she had to be a bit cruel if she had to demolish this calmness.

"You wear *swadeshi* clothes but are prepared to send your children to *videshi* schools? Is this your idea of *swadeshi*? Why don't you banish your *angrezi* ideas from your head instead of banishing their clothes from your skin?"

She paused for effect.

"After what they did to your father, all that suffering, are you prepared to send Shree to be moulded by them?"

Radha was encouraged by the effect it had on her husband. He looked somewhat angry now. She continued, "We may wear French clips, and English brocades and use 'Made in England' scissors but at heart we are Indian. My *sanskars* are Indian and it is our duty to preserve them. Very soon our children will eat with their shoes on from a common container, like our cows and horses eat. What an insult to *Anna Devta!*"

Radha stopped but started once again when she thought of something, "And I just don't like the way their women dress, bare legs for everyone to see!" She shrugged her shoulders vigorously to stress her point.

Girdhar pondered over the matter for a few days but finally decided to enrol Shree in the *Isaai School.*

The only explanation he gave Radha was that the missionaries had come to their country with a different purpose than those who ruled India.

On the fifth day, Shree returned from school and went straight up searching for Pusibai. She had an iron tong in her hand with which she was turning the coals. The undersides shone brightly, occasionally spitting sparks. Shree stood next to her, stuck his fingers to his head to form two imaginary ears and started singing—"Pusibai, Pusibai where have you been?

I have been to London to look at the Queen.

Pusibai, Pusibai what did you do there?"

Pusibai didn't understand a word, but she knew it wasn't complimentary. She ran with her tongs raised like a sword to get hold of Shree. But he had vanished.

The coals laughed merrily.

The family noticed Jagannath go frail. He grew weaker both in body and in spirit. Girdhar saw him detached and aloof. Now he seldom made inquiries about business activities. It worried Girdhar. Something was definitely wrong. Business was his life. He had nurtured it and it flourished under him ever since his father's death. Then he had supervised his son's every business move. Why did he let go now? It disturbed him.

He knew his father had never really recovered ever since he returned from hiding. The constant wandering from place to place had taken a toll on his health. He looked exhausted and worn out. Girdhar wondered whether it was the guilt of not standing by his friend that was slowly withering him away or whether it was a physical ailment. He thought and hoped that time would gently heal his father's body and spirit, but it never did.

Jagannath died one day, complaining of a severe pain in his chest. The women believed that some envious person had cast an evil spell on him, otherwise healthy people don't just die like that. His was no age to die. He had yet to see his grandchildren's marriage and play with their children.

His guidance was still essential for the family.

Girdhar missed his reassuring presence. He felt abandoned and alone. Like a roof being ripped off one's head rendering him exposed and vulnerable. Munimji stood by him and gave him courage.

Even then, while at work he often asked himself, "Would father approve of this, or not? Would this make him angry?"

Jagannath lived in Krishna's heart and Girdhar's mind.

Sunken eyes, frail body, a voice barely audible. No, this was not Krishna's Dadaji. A devastated Krishna tried hard to erase this frame. Instead, she hung a picture of Dadaji wearing a crisp white *dhoti*, walking erect, eyes smiling at her, lips calling out 'Krishna' on the walls of her memory. She looked at it for solace whenever the pain became unbearable. Who would make up excuses for her and rescue her from maa's scolding and from Munimji's terrifying, red eyes?

VII
Girdhar : 1940

Solapur was preparing for the Municipal elections. Girdhar was contesting for the President's post. The men's *baithak* was bustling with activity. Rukmini and Shree hung around on the pretext of serving water to the over used hoarse throats or lemon sherbet for the tired bodies.

They saw their father's supporters leave after long hours of discussions. They left behind *paan* and tobacco stains on spotless white sheets. Rukmini noticed their *kurtas* were yellower than the sheets. The *dhobi* bleached the sheets white again.

Rukmini was curious. She asked her father how one votes.

"There are three of us contesting. Each has a symbol," he explained.

"What's yours?"

"A kneeling Hanuman"

"Oh! That will prove lucky!"

"Each voter has to put three crosses. He can do so in any way he chooses, by putting a cross on each, or two crosses on one symbol and one on the other, or putting all the three for one contestant," Girdhar explained to his attentive daughter.

"And the one who gets the maximum crosses wins!"

"That's right."

"Can the women vote?"

"Yes, but they hardly come. But this time we'll encourage them to come out and vote."

"Your opponent is a Maharashtrian?" Rukmini asked.

"Yes"

"Their women will come. Our Marwari women won't."

Girdhar was struck by his daughter's clarity of mind. He

knew it was true, and he had discussed it with his supporters. He had sought Radha's help in canvassing. She had refused. She couldn't possibly go door to door begging for votes. She agreed to talk to women in temples, functions and during social visits. Girdhar decided to request the men to get their wives along to vote.

The Election Day arrived with Girdhar very anxious and wondering if he had done the right thing by contesting. His family name was at stake and it would be embarrassing if he lost. Rukmini wore her best skirt and blouse. She put a chord through the fountain pen clip and slipped it around her neck. Girdhar put one of his white Gandhi *topees* on her head and looked admiringly at one of his most ardent fans. She smiled, displaying her new permanent teeth, which seemed too big for her small face. She looked like a party worker now. She adjusted the Gandhi *topee* at a slight tilt and set off with her father.

Till two in the afternoon there weren't any women in sight. Rukmini was growing impatient. Her targets hadn't arrived and she was disappointed. Then they came in groups or with their husbands and sons. As soon as she spotted Marwari women, recognising them by their distinct voluminous *ghagras*, she led them to the women's area.

"Do you know what you have to do?"

Most often it was a hesitant "no".

"I'll tell you, just put three crosses next to Hanumanji, he'll bless you."

Some hadn't held a pen all their lives.

She offered them her services "Take me inside along with you, I'll show you." Once inside, she put the crosses herself and asked the women to put it in the ballot box.

Quietly, tirelessly she went about her job unnoticed. Her innocent presence was unobjectionable. She was like any other child who had accompanied her parent to watch *Ramlila* or a *Ganpati* procession. Only Girdhar realised what she had done for him. Her efforts paid off. Girdhar won and became the

President of the Municipal Corporation. Rukmini learnt a lesson that would give her entire life direction and meaning.

She impressed upon her little mind that ignorance was a curse.

It was worse than being a woman.

Worst was being an ignorant woman.

Rukmini arrived on the terrace where Shree was waiting for her. His mouth fell open when he saw her in his white shirt and loose *khaki* shorts. Her thick black plait ended with a red ribbon. It divided her slender shoulders and back. Rukmini looked up at a blue speck in the sky that was their kite. Her eyes narrowed into slits as she focussed but her smile was broad. Shree stood nearby with the *chakri* between his two thumbs and fingers. His smile was broader.

Shree too had inherited Kesar maa's large eyes and chiselled nose, but he was much darker. He looked tough and rugged. He had thick hair, which he oiled and neatly combed back away from his forehead. He had large ears prominently visible from any angle. He hung around Rukmini and followed her faithfully.

Three kites had laid down their lives to the glass laced thread. The whole morning they had pounded glass and mixed it with gum. This they coated on a thick thread and dried it in the sun. Both had bruises on their palms.

The three kites floated aimlessly before being grabbed by clapping children in the street below. They both rejoiced at the prize. But Gopu's red kite was still flying high, beckoning and teasing them. They had to take it. Gopu had severed many of their kites. It had to be avenged. Gopu laughed from the terrace opposite their's. His sniggering had to vanish. With the concentration of a surgeon, Rukmini pulled her kite taut over Gopu's and crossed his thread. She jerked her glass-coated thread, once, twice, thrice and neatly cut her opponent's thread.

Shree threw the *chakri* down and clapped his hands. The children below applauded too. Rukmini saw Gopu's smile disappear, and then him. The terrace opposite was empty. She held the thread of her victorious kite like a trophy for everyone to see.

Dhum...

The harsh impact on her back thrust her forward. She nearly fell. Staggering, she turned around and saw her mother. Her hands raised to strike... again. Her eyes spat fire. The uncut diamonds studded in the "bor" caught the sun and reflected it angrily.

"You insolent child—" she screamed—"is this all I could instil in you? To behave like a spoilt brat? How dare you stand on my terrace and tease boys? Was I dead that you had no fear of me? That's what the people are going to say, was the mother dead that the girl went berserk?"

Rukmini sensed that there was no point arguing today. She left the string and ran down the stairs. Hot tears scalded her soft cheeks. She thumped down the wooden stairs. Munimji looked up and saw an angry Rukmini rushing down. He guessed there had been a war. Oh! His little soldier has had a skirmish and that too, dressed in a uniform! He smiled to himself on seeing Rukmini in loose, khaki shorts. He didn't stop her. Just signalled a servant to follow her. He knew where she would go.

The wind was strong and the kite was still flying. Shree had just weighed down the *chakri* with his right foot.

By the time she reached Kesar maa, her eyes were red, cheeks flushed, her face wet and nose running.

Kesar maa stuck her needle to the wrong side of the *duree* she was sitting on. She put down the new net dress she was making for Gopal, especially for the summer. Her moving lips stopped chanting as she turned her attention towards Rukmini. Rukmini hid her face in her lap.

"I will never go home again. Maa gets angry at stupid things and hits me."

Kesar maa let her cry. When she was quieter, she asked, "Did your mother get angry because you wore Shree's clothes?"

"No, because I was flying kites. And we were happy when we cut Gopu's kite. Maa can't see us laugh and play."

Her grandmother smiled to herself. She understood the predicament her daughter was in. She was caught between the rules laid down for girls by the society and her daughter who refused to be bound by them. The anger and frustration was more due to Radha's own incompetence to harness a ten-year-old rather than Rukmini's lack of discipline. Solving problems with Munimji or flying kites weren't much of a sin. But her exuberance and fearlessness certainly were.

Girls ought to be like cows—meek, and gentle. Tied all their lives to a hook—ungrudgingly.

Kesar maa wiped the tears with her cotton sari.

"Why do you always infuriate your mother? Krishna never gets any scolding, why?"

Rukmini stopped crying. Defiant and poised, she retorted.

"That's because Jiji does only what Maa wants her to do. Maa asks her to miss school, she misses it. Maa asks to stitch and sew, she does just that till her fingers bleed. Haven't you seen Jiji's fingers? If I listen to Maa, I'll have bleeding fingers too."

"But you do have bruised hands. What have you been doing ?" Kesar maa had noticed Rukmini's cuts and bruises.

Rukmini grinned sheepishly and explained the entire kite experience. Her grandmother smiled too.

"Nanima, Gopu had been cutting our kites every day. We had to do something about it, isn't it? So we mixed pounded glass in gum and coated our thread. You should have seen how neatly we cut his kite. It was worth all these bruises."

"You don't mind these wounds, but you mind the pricks that needlework gives you." Her grandmother couldn't help teasing her. But, Rukmini was very serious.

"Nanima I want to do what I like, not what others want

me to do."

"I know that, always try to strike a balance between what you want, and what others expect of you."

Kesar maa gently lifted strands of hair that had stuck on Rukmini's wet cheeks and forehead.

"You must be hungry after a long afternoon, will you eat something?" She asked.

"Yes, I'll have the almond and saffron milk you make every afternoon for Gopal. Is the *bhog* ready?"

The milk was still behind the curtain before Gopal. Kesar maa picked up the milk, tinted with saffron and floating almonds.

Rukmini drank the milk and chewed the almonds with relish.

For three days she remained with her grandmother, enjoying all the *prasad* and Nanima's attention.

"I won't go to maa again," she told her grandmother.

"*Nahi, beta!* Never be so angry with your mother. You must understand that whatever she does is for your good."

Rukmini didn't believe that her mother's anger did her any good, but she kept quiet for her grandmother's sake.

Krishna had come to see her. Finally Girdhar came to fetch her and took her home. Radha still didn't speak to her.

VIII
Krishna-Rukmini—The Picnic

The whole school was excited. The girls were going on a picnic. For most of the girls who had never stepped out of town, the twenty kilometres of travel was exciting enough. Elaborate plans were made and each was allotted a food item. They had to leave by seven the next day.

Radha was still angry. Krishna was too scared to ask her mother to pack tiffin for them and Rukmini was too proud. The cook and Pusibai wouldn't make a thing unless their mother gave the sanction.

"I won't go without the *purees*, what will the teachers say? It's better we don't go at all." Krishna always resigned to her fate.

"Let me think—we'll find a way out."

The girls rose early that day and were ready by six. Radha was bathing. The sisters left a message with Pusibai, that they had left for the picnic.

"But what about the *purees?*" Krishna enquired.

"Come on! I have an idea."

She and Krishna went straight to Kesar maa. She was in the *puja-room*, bathing Gopal.

'Nanima, we are going on a picnic, can you give us *prasad?* Lots of it, for all my friends?"

Kesar maa asked them to wait.

"No, we just can't wait today. We'll be left behind," Rukmini tried to sound urgent.

She knew Nanima would never refuse. She packed all the *prasad* she had in a bamboo basket and tied it in a clean cloth. She knotted it on top and handed it over to the girls. The coachman dropped them to school.

"My mother will send the tiffin by car with our servant. It wasn't ready," Rukmini informed her teacher. He seemed convinced. It was quite possible for a rich *seth's* daughter to be accompanied by her own escort. Krishna marvelled at the way her sister sailed through difficult situations.

The train chugged on slowly, while the girls sang and chattered.

"Masterji, my grandmother has sent *prasad* for all of you." She and Krishna distributed the *pedhas, laddus, nariyal burfis,* fried peanuts and potato chips. They ate till the basket was empty. It was an unexpected feast and all of them thoroughly enjoyed it.

It was late afternoon and everyone was hungry, but there was no sign of Rukmini's tiffin. Rukmini pretended to be genuinely worried. Her teacher consoled her "Don't worry, there are other girls who have brought *purees*. Something must have gone wrong."

Krishna sighed in utter relief. Rukmini smiled a mischievous smile.

IX

Krishna-Ram : 1941

Krishna had grown taller—taller than her mother. Marwari mothers were paranoid about their daughters growing tall, about their attaining puberty, about their obvious signs of growing up. Radha was no exception. She voiced her apprehensions and fears about Krishna growing up so soon. Krishna tried to look as inconspicuous as possible and hunched to look smaller. Girdhar had always ignored Radha's queries regarding Krishna's marriage. Radha broached the topic again, Girdhar pretended to sleep.

She was annoyed.

"How can you sleep so soundly when you have a marriageable daughter growing as tall as a pillar? Men lose their sleep just worrying over this."

Radha expected him to respond. He did.

"What do you expect me to do?"

"What do you mean, what are you supposed to do?" she snapped.

"What do fathers do? Don't you know?"

"She's young yet we'll see, after a few months."

"Hai Ram! Young? She's nearly fourteen, how long will you keep her?"

"I wish, forever," Girdhar replied, eyes moist.

Radha softened.

"I know you love your daughters more than anything else but still you cannot evade the truth. Sooner or later, daughters have to go."

"I know," he replied simply.

"People have started talking. They all feel you have pampered them too much."

"You too feel the same way, don't you?"

Radha avoided answering it directly.

"It's more painful to part if you are so emotionally attached."

"So, what we do is deny them their right to be loved? Daughters are so lovable, so caring, why are we in such a haste to send them away?" Girdhar argued.

Radha didn't want the situation to turn emotional. She wanted a practical solution.

"Fourteen? You call it haste? You are already late. You are fortunate, people are asking for your daughter's hand, otherwise you have fathers wearing their soles out to find a suitable match for their poor daughters."

The long drawn discussion ended with a final decision. Munimji treated like an elder of the house would go on a tour. He would visit and inspect prospective grooms, and their social standing. Girdhar would then finalise the best proposal himself.

Munimji set out on an auspicious day. It would take him almost a month. His luggage had photographs of Krishna, which would be given only if he approved of somebody. He was aware of the responsibility he had to shoulder and assured Girdhar that he would do his best. Like Sethji would have, for his favourite granddaughter.

He returned after a tiring journey and told Girdhar that he had approved of a family of a good reputation and considerable wealth. They owned silk mills and that he had already fixed Krishna's marriage with their son. In fact they were very keen to associate themselves with 'our' family.

Girdhar was in a dilemma. Radha was apprehensive.

"What was the hurry? He could have at least sought your approval. He shouldn't have decided Krishna's fate so hastily." Radha was tense and angry.

"Nothing can be done now. He has given his word on our behalf. Girdhar tried his best to convince himself and Radha.

"But you needn't worry. I won't finalise anything till I have met the 'boy'."

Something struck Radha, "You mean to say..."

"The boy was not there; he was away with his maternal grandparents," Girdhar said, not letting her complete the sentence.

"Oh my God!" was all Radha could manage to say for a while.

Finally, she broke the silence.

"Gone are the days when, such marriages were made," she said thoughtfully.

"We should at least see the boy first before we hand over our daughter to him." It still didn't occur to her that Krishna might want to see the 'boy' she was going to marry.

Girdhar approved of the match Munimji had arranged. There was no reason to object. The boy was called Ram. His father and uncles had come and approved of Krishna. Krishna was informed; she was engaged to be married.

Stealthily Krishna went into her mother's room. Her heart beat madly and her mouth was dry. Slowly she opened the cupboard and groped under the clothes. She found it and a hundred thoughts raced through her mind.

It took her a moment to muster courage to turn the photograph over.

There he was—looking away from her (why couldn't he look her way?).

Crisp *dhoti* and shiny brown shoes. Elbows rested on a high three-legged stool with a stack of three thick books. He rested his elbows on them (as if he had just finished reading them all).

There was a halo around his head (like the one Lord Rama had in one of the paintings in their house).

Krishna read the studio's name which was carefully hand painted on the right hand corner.

An umbrella rested in the other corner (what a useless prop!).

He was neither dark, nor flat nosed, nor thick lipped and wasn't squint-eyed like Rukmini told her he was. In fact she thought he was quite good looking. A straight nose with well defined nostrils, soft small eyes and a pleasing smile.

Munimji was not the villain she thought him to be.

She hurriedly shoved the photograph back and left the room with a great sense of relief. All she knew about him was that he was in the tenth standard and wanted to study engineering. Baba was very pleased about him being educated.

She was pleased about his looks.

Krishna was fourteen now, much older than Radha wanted her to be. The world war had left food scarce and prices soaring. There were stringent laws on people congregating and on hosting feasts. No more than twenty-five people could be fed at a time. Organising a wedding in such circumstances was difficult. Girdhar decided to wait for a few months.

Radha forbade Krishna to go to school.

"Daughters from respectable families don't wander about aimlessly," she declared. Krishna was now being trained to be a good *bahu*.

Rukmini had protested. If not in school Jiji should at least have a teacher at home. Radha relented and a *masterji* gave her private tutions. He made her memorise Sanskrit *shlokas* whose meaning he himself didn't understand. Radha made Krishna embroider her own wedding trousseau and stitch her own blouses. The more she learnt the happier she would be, Radha had repeatedly told Krishna. It was not Krishna's disposition to question anything so she never asked how learning these things would make her happy in the future. Her silence was an indication that Radha had moulded her daughter 'properly'. She was confident that her daughter would have no difficulty adjusting in her husband's household. She was immensely proud of her daughter.

Nanima taught Krishna to make delicious sweets. She instilled in her the power of prayer. Krishna believed her when her grandmother said that Gopal's benevolence had fetched her a good husband. Now she should fast and pray for his happiness and long life.

Krishna was bathing Gopal with *panchamrit*, one day. He sat on a silver platter, smiling mischievously, as usual. After his *abhishek,* he would shine and smell of honey and *mogra* perfumes. Krishna gently lifted him and placed him on her palm. She dried him with a soft cloth, careful not to hurt him with her nails. She wiped his tiny eyes and crevices of his small round face.

"Tell me Nanima, why doesn't Maa do so much for Gopal? A Brahmini performs our *puja*. Maa never bathes or makes anything for our Gopal," Krishna asked her grandmother.

Kesar maa tried to shrug off her inquiry lightly—"Oh, she's a busy housewife. She has a big household to look after. Husband, children and relatives. I was less troubled."

She had convinced Krishna, but Kesar maa knew it was not the entire truth. Gopal was always Radha's rival, someone she competed with. Nobody could love a rival. He not only stole butter in the stories her mother told her, but also stole her mother's attention, and affection. He stole what was rightfully hers, and she resented it. That was the truth.

Kesar maa knew Radha celebrated *Janamashtmi* as a ritual, but she never would see Gopal as she saw him—Supreme Lord himself, but who also needed all the pampering and fussing of a toddler. Who never grew up, never complained—just smiled his benevolent smile.

While Krishna was being trained upstairs, Rukmini was arguing with Munimji.

"Munimji Dadaji, it's not fair at all. When I can do the sums better than Shree, why is it that you refuse to teach me further? I want to learn how to calculate interest and compound interest."

She was offended when Munimji told her not to come to him any more. She had learnt enough mathematics to see her through life and that she should now learn "other things" from her mother. He added that he would now only groom Shree. He would use it in future. What would Rukmini do with it anyway?

Rukmini listened, hurt and angry. The tears welled in her large eyes and Munimji looked blurred.

How could he be so mean she thought, she was his favourite. Or was it something she only imagined?

Krishna was Nanima's favourite. Shree was everybody's pet, nobody really loved or even wanted her. She knew how everybody was disappointed when she was born. She had heard stories about it. She chose not to believe them—but it was the truth.

The thought made her sob inconsolably.

"Oh dear! You don't cry so easily, what's wrong with you today?" Munimji had sensed the hurt. He thought of something to distract her. He knew she couldn't bear grudges for long.

"Come, come, I'll ask you some riddles. Let's see if you can give me the answers correctly."

"I am not interested in riddles, will you let me come to you with Shree or not?" Rukmini wasn't relenting today.

Munimji saw the determination in her eyes. Through the tears her gaze was steady and confident. What would she do if Munimji refused, she wondered. She didn't know. No but, she wouldn't show she was unsure. Her face would reflect only her confidence. She looked straight into his eyes, and waited for his answer.

Munimji fidgeted. He looked uncomfortable, but Rukmini waited with gaze unmoving and fixed. The tears were still in them, but the determination on her face had returned.

He thought of a safe way out. "All right, but I'll ask your father first—if he refuses..."

Rukmini smiled even before he could complete his sentence. She knew *Baba* would never refuse. They both knew.

Rukmini wiped her tears with the back of her hands and said, "You can ask the riddles now, if you wish."

Munimji smiled—exposing his tobacco stained teeth, each tooth outlined by a dark brown line.

"You always get what you want, don't you?" He said.

"No I don't, I have to fight for it."

Rukmini smiled, "You can ask me the riddles now," she said again, somewhat impishly.

The riddles of Rajasthan have the unique quality of revealing its social fabric, its customs, rituals and beliefs. They subtly speak of the social behaviour.

Munimji knew scores of them and asked them, very often befitting the situation. Rukmini was by now smiling and happy, troubles put away far behind.

Rukmini see if you can guess this one,

Pan sade, Ghoda ade,
Vidya Beeser jaye.
Khe mein Roto bal gayo,
Kyon chela kin thai.

[The betel leaf rots, the horse becomes stubborn and won't run, knowledge acquired is lost, the bread on the coal burns, tell me, when does all this happen?]

Rukmini looked foxed, she said, "I don't know."

"Hmmm. See all this can happen if you don't turn these things over, or if you don't revise."

"Oh yes!" Rukmini said brightly. Of course, *paan* leaves have to be turned over every day otherwise they become yellow and the *roti* has to be turned over on the coals or it will burn, and knowledge has to be revised..."

She stopped short, tiny folds appeared between her

eyebrows. Obviously something bothered her.

"Then why did you not want me to learn more maths? Wouldn't I have forgotten everything I learnt?"

"Forget that now. I'll ask you another one, let's see if you can guess this one." Munimji tactfully evaded her query

He continued in his chaste Marwari,

Oont charyo oti,
Kambar bandho sheti.
Aage Baithi hai Jhinki,
Thanke ben laage ki beti?
Na mhari ben lage, Na mhari beti,
Iri sasu—mhari sasu,
Sagi maa Beti.

[A man asks a *seth* astride a camel, "Is the woman sitting before you your sister or your daughter?"

He replies, "She isn't my sister nor is she my daughter, but her mother-in-law and my mother-in-law are real mother and daughter."]

Munimji asked Rukmini how the man and woman on the camel were related. Rukmini made a face and shrugged her shoulders in denial.

"This one is really difficult. I don't like these complicated ones. Give me something to calculate."

Then, after a moment of thought, she asked, "Could I ask Maa, she'll know it surely?"

Munimji let her go readily. He wanted to get back to work now. The riddle would keep her away for a while.

But she was back within a few minutes, with a broad smile, all over her expressive face. "Ma solved it, the woman is the man's daughter-in-law."

Munimji was pleased. "You are so much like your mother, aren't you? Smart and intelligent."

"What about my sums now?" Munimji shook his head in resignation. She was impossible.

And so Munimji taught her and Shree to calculate simple

interest. When both had learnt the formula and practised several sums, Munimji told them one day, "Children, it is of utmost importance for you to understand, that in business you should keep a very close watch on the interest you pay. We pay interest on loans, and also on delayed payments. Bad businessmen pay so much interest that in the end they realise it has gradually consumed most of the profit. So always refrain from paying interest. A shrewd businessman should manage his finance so that he pays minimum interest. Remember that a man can labour and earn during the day, but interest earns day and night, it never rests. It takes no holidays. Do you follow me?" Munimji asked when he saw two blank faces.

The children shook their heads in denial.

"Not entirely," Shree said.

"All right let me explain, suppose you have taken a loan of Rs. 100 from 'X'. You pay an interest of say 5 per cent per year. So every year you pay Rs. 5 to 'X' as simple interest. Now, if you don't repay the loan, then the next year you pay interest on Rs. 105. This is compound interest. So you see how silently it is working? Each year your amount increases and also your interest. So always keep an eye on the interest you are paying. It was the first important thing I learnt in business."

" That was great, who taught you all this?"

"My father."

"And Him."

"His father," he smiled. I never attended school."

"You mean to say that you keep such complicated accounts even though you never went to school?" Rukmini was wide eyed with surprise.

"My father was very strict where arithmetic was concerned. One wrong sum would mean a harsh whack on our palms. His *chhadi* would leave our palms red and swollen. We had no option but to do our sums right. But I don't regret it now. It has made me into a responsible *munim.* I do not know what I would have done for a living otherwise."

"Now will you let me return to my work? Run along you two."

They both scampered away.

The three children pestered their grandmother and mother to tell them stories. They heard stories of Lord Krishna and Lord Ram and of the valiant queens of Rajasthan and ardent devotees like Mirabai and Tulsidas. Their sparkling eyes and curious faces held the same fascination even if the stories were told over and over again. All listened with rapt attention, even forgetting to blink. Good would prevail over evil, but each child perceived the story differently.

The actual fight between the good and the bad excited Shree. He wanted to hear details of how Ram's arrows pierced Ravan or how Lakshman cut off Shurphanka's nose. Krishna was impressed by the absolute devotion of Shabree and Mirabai and Sita's sacrifices. Rukmini marvelled at Kevat's brilliance, how he cleverly made Lord Ram do exactly what he wanted. She admired Lord Krishna's diplomatic moves, which resulted in the *Mahabharat* and eventually the victory of intelligence over physical strength.

It was 2.30 pm in the afternoon. The food in Munimji's stomach always made him drowsy. Rukmini and Shree saw his eyes closing involuntarily. They knew he would recline on the heavy bolsters for his afternoon siesta. They also knew he would wave them away with his ink stained hands.

He was most vulnerable at this time of the day.

"Can we eat some *churan*?" Shree asked.

Munimji pointed towards his desk, nodded and closed his eyes. Shree opened it, looked in and surveyed the inkpots, penholders, stamps and coins that were arranged neatly in their compartments. He located the familiar *churan* bottles and felt his mouth water. He picked up the newest container and inspected it. Baba must have got it from Mumbai, he assumed. Quickly he opened it. The ball of the *churan* seemed unusually big. The colour was different too. It was rolled in silver foil.

"Queer," both said, but it looked delicious. There was no harm in eating it. He handed over one to Rukmini and put one in his mouth. Both looked at each other, raising their eyebrows. Rukmini crinkled her nose and shook her head.

"It isn't tasty," she meant to say. Shree agreed.

"Forget it, let's go," Rukmini said. "I wonder if Baba knows how ghastly this tastes."

"We'll let him know."

Rukmini held her brother's hand and pulled him along. Both sat on the fountain edge wondering what to do.

"Marbles?" Shree asked.

"Hmmm, All right, let's go."

Shree dug out a handful of marbles from his pockets and went out of the house. But something was wrong. Both felt their tongues go dry.

"Are you thirsty?" Shree asked.

"Yes, come, let's go in."

By the time they drank water the duo felt something was terribly wrong.

"Someone's pulling my tongue," Shree said.

"Mine too, from the inside."

"What could it be?" Shree asked, looking quite frightened now.

"*Bhoot,*" she couldn't help teasing though she was scared herself.

Their tongues got heavier and their legs weighed a ton. Arms were getting immobile.

"Do you think it's the *churan* we ate?" Rukmini looked at Shree with frightened eyes.

"What do we do now?" Shree wanted to cry but was putting on a brave front.

"Jiji," Rukmini called out as soon as she located Krishna. Climbing the stairs had posed a greater threat than the Himalayas. They saw Krishna with her back resting on the wall, knees up and elbows resting on them. She played with her four gold bangles. Up the arm, and then down again to the wrist. She was so engrossed that she didn't hear her siblings approach her.

"Jiji," they both called out softly. Krishna looked up, "*Haan*?"

Both fell silent, too scared to speak up.

"I think we are both going to die," Rukmini finally said with great difficulty.

"What?" She asked alarmed. "What are you saying, you stupid things?"

"We ate something from Munimji's desk, it looked like *churan*. But it wasn't."

Krishna noticed that their speech was now slurred and slow, as though somebody had tied their tongues. But it could be one of their pranks she thought. They were always up to something silly. She decided to wait and see what they would do next. Shree held up his hand.

"See, our fingers are locked, they won't disengage."

Both demonstrated, how their fingers would not unlock.

Krishna held their wrists and pulled them apart quite effortlessly.

"Now will you stop this *natak*?" She said angrily. "Or I'll call somebody."

Rukmini slumped to the floor, watery eyed. Shree followed suit. Both sat on the ground with their legs spread straight in front of them. Both looked up, desperately trying to say something.

"J-i-j-i, t-h-e-r-e a-r-e c-r-a-m-p-s i-n m-y s-t-o-m-a-c-h." Rukmini implored.

"M-i-n-e t-o-o." Shree repeated.

Krishna realised something was indeed wrong. They

couldn't have possibly put up an act for so long.

"I'll call Maa", she said.

"No." Both said in unison. "She'll kill us, before we die of this."

"All right, don't move from here, I'll go and call someone."

Rukmini laughed at her sister's statement.

"I-s-n-t J-i-j-i a-c-t-i-n-g f-u-n-n-y? W-e c-a-n't m-o-v-e a-n-y-w-a-y-," she told Shree. He nodded in approval.

Krishna ran upstairs. She stumbled over her sari pleats and fell. It irritated her now. This sari was such a bother. But Maa wouldn't listen. She made her wear it every day now. Pusibai was sleeping, her face covered with her *pallav*.

Krishna decided not to disturb her. She would get angry, she knew. Maharaj sat lazily, smoking a *bidi*. She quickly explained that Rukmini and Shree were in trouble. She dragged a reluctant, not-pleased-to-be-disturbed man, to where both Rukmini and Shree were sitting. She found them just as she had left them. Both were talking incessantly.

Maharaj had one look at them and knew what was wrong.

"You have eaten *bhang* you fools. Get up, I'll give you lemon juice, you'll be all right then."

Shri put his palms flat on the floor and made an effort to rise.

"B-u-t I a-m s-t-u-c-k t-o t-h-e f-l-o-o-r. I c-a-n't g-e-t u-p." Shree declared.

"Y-e-s! W-e a-r-e! H-o-n-e-s-t-l-y!" Rukmini tried to convince.

"J-i-j-i a-s-k-e-d u-s n-o-t t-o m-o-v-e s-o w-e g-o-t s-t-u-c-k." Shree slurred.

They made a funny sight. They sat with their legs in front of them, believing that they were stuck to the ground. Krishna held her stomach, doubled over and laughed till her eyes watered. Maharaj gave a wide grin. Rukmini and Shree looked up with a questioning look. What was wrong? Why was Krishna laughing? Rukmini laughed first, Shree followed. None of them realised the commotion they were creating.

They slowly drew a small crowd, around them. Like the *madari* who attracts an audience, with the distinct sound of the *damru*. There was loud laughter and everybody poked fun at them. Then suddenly Radha arrived on the scene. It took her a few moments to register what exactly was happening. She looked at them sternly and the children froze. The crowd around them thinned, like the audience of the *madari*, who slip away quickly as soon as he circulates his bowl for money.

Radha was alone with the children.

"Do you know the scene you are creating? You can be heard across the street. People must be wondering what this din is all about. Who gave you the *bhang* to eat in the first place?"

Radha was trying not to be angry with her two helpless children. But her voice gave her away.

Rukmini mustered courage by now. She was aware that everybody was laughing at them because of their behaviour. She felt ashamed. She prepared herself to sound sensible, at least for her mother. But something blocked her mind. It took a great effort to articulate an answer. She pooled in all her concentration, but all she could manage was, "Maa, we are stuck to the ground. Believe me, and I am hungry."

"Me too," Shree added.

Rukmini saw her mother laugh too. It hurt her and she felt the tears fill her eyes. She fought to banish them. She didn't want to be laughed at, but she didn't want to be pitied either. She heard her mother give instructions to the cook to feed them, and to Pusibai to look after them, and then leave the room.

The children ate like hogs, their hunger insatiable. Finally Maharaj told them that they should stop eating or they would fall ill.

Shree said it was difficult to sleep with an empty stomach. Rukmini agreed.

Maharaj had laughed again.

Rukmini slept on the floor where they had been sitting the whole afternoon. (Because she was stuck to the floor).

Shree slept on the floor too, out of sheer exhaustion (and because he was stuck too) wondering why they were not fed. Elders could be so cruel!

They woke up late the next morning, sheepish and guilty. They avoided every living creature in the household. Both ran away into the orchards, swearing never to touch Munimji's deadly desk again.

Shree and Rukmini were up a guava tree, dropping sweet ripe fruits on the ground. Yesterday's troubles were behind them and they laughed at the two *koels* on the tree. Each answered the other's call with equal zeal and loyalty. It intrigued the children.

"Do you think they can understand each other?" Shree asked his sister.

"I think they do but I wonder whether they sing to the other or talk to each other."

"I am sure they sing," Shree said, sounding very wise. It was rare that he caught his sister unsure about anything. He didn't want to miss the opportunity to sound more intelligent. But her thoughts scampered elsewhere.

"You know Shree, my friend went to the cinema, she said. People even sing in them."

"How can they?" he asked in utter amazement.

"Don't know, but she said the voice came from a box behind them."

"Wish we could see it."

"Don't even think of it. Maa will thrash us if she hears of it."

"Let's go on the sly."

"Maa says cinema is not for decent people."

"So does that mean your friend is not decent?"

"It does not mean that. But there are many people who do

not approve of going to the cinema. Our parents too believe that, so we just have to listen to them."

Shree shrugged.

Then Rukmini remembered something, and her face brightened.

"Shree, you know one of my classmates has left school to become an actress."

"Who?" His eyes growing wider.

"Shashikala."

"Her parents allowed her to go?"

"Guess so, she's is in Mumbai now acting in the cinema."

"She must be enjoying herself in Mumbai, *nahi*?" Shree said biting his lower lip with his upper teeth.

"How do we know? Someone told me its hard work."

"What? Singing songs? I could do that the whole day," Shree declared.

"They don't really sing songs, someone else sings for them."

Rukmini had gathered the information from one of her friends whose mother was a classical singer.

"Now stop it Jiji, you just said they sing in films, then you say someone else ....are you making a fool of me?"

Both were still up the tree, like two chattering monkeys. The *koels* were still singing, alternately.

Rukmini burst out laughing seeing her brother cross and confused. She nearly lost her balance and caught hold of a branch.

" Leave it Shree, you won't understand, you are too small for all these things," Rukmini teased.

Shree frowned and turned away to show his displeasure.

The *koels* caught her attention again.

"Don't they ever get tired and hoarse," Rukmini thought. "They have so much to tell each other, wonder what it could be? Sorrows? Joys?" She wondered.

It was late afternoon—milk-time. "They had better hurry up," she told Shree before Maa missed them. As she climbed down her skirt got caught on the bark of the tree and she heard the *"trrrr"* distinctly.

"Oh no; more work for Jiji."

They swallowed the milk, hungry after a tiring afternoon outside. She held out two ripe guavas for Krishna and said, "They are very sweet, eat them."

Krishna took them, and polished them till they shone a lovely green. She dug her teeth into the juicy fruit. "Ruku, it's delicious."

"Jiji, I tore my skirt on the tree. Will you stitch it for me?" Krishna felt sorry for her sister. It was one of the last three skirts she had left now. All were fraying at the hem. Maa had warned her to start wearing saris. She was old enough to do so. Grown up girls didn't go around wearing a skirt and a blouse. Maa had told her to put away all her skirts.

Rukmini had refused. She wasn't going to school in a sari. None of her classmates wore a sari, she argued.

Maa said, she could stop going to school then. It was doing nothing good to her, anyway. It was making her headstrong and argumentative.

Rukmini declared she would go to school, in a skirt, no matter what.

Maa announced she would stop getting any new skirts made for her. She would see how long Rukmini could carry on.

So now Rukmini was left with three old skirts and worn out blouses.

Krishna stitched the skirt as best as she could.

Rukmini wore it again with her usual pride. It didn't bother her when her classmates teased her about it, or when she could feel her teachers wondering why, the daughter of a rich *seth* was wearing worn out clothes to school.

Girdhar noticed her torn skirt one day and was sympathetic when Rukmini told him Maa wasn't making new skirts for her. He took her shopping and bought the best silk, brocade and finest cottons with woven borders. The family tailor was summoned and he asked him to stitch clothes for Rukmini immediately. Rukmini was now the best-dressed girl in school, but it pained her to see her mother silent and hurt. She had won a battle for herself, but couldn't rejoice.

Radha had kept quiet throughout, but hell broke loose when Girdhar bought a sari for Krishna from Mumbai.

"A sari for Rs. 5?" she had asked in astonishment.

"You are spoiling the girls. You will regret later, when they won't get all this at their in-laws' house. Nobody is going to spend such princely sums to please your daughters. They will be unhappy and what will you do then?"

Radha rarely confronted Girdhar so angrily. He knew he had hurt her when he got the new skirts for Rukmini. But he couldn't bear to see his daughter in tatters.

"I know nobody is going to spend so much on them. That's precisely why I want to give them the best I can," Girdhar said, his voice breaking with emotion. "You don't know what the future holds for them, do you? At least we can give them a happy present."

Radha hadn't argued then. She missed her father like she had never missed before. He must have loved her the same way, she thought. Why couldn't she love her children so passionately, she wondered. Sometimes this thought disturbed her to the point of tears. Why couldn't she just gather her children in her arms and show her love? Demonstration of anger, hate and love was not the right behaviour. It was instilled in her so deeply that it was difficult to disregard it now. She would be called shameless so she crushed her desire to share any physical bond with her own children. Sometimes her helplessness and frustration would show up as anger, ironically against the very children she wanted to love so much. For the sole reason, that they were the only ones on whom she could direct her wrath. The rest of the household (including the servants) was to be respected. A virtuous daughter-in-law couldn't possibly show her displeasure. So it was Girdhar in the privacy of her bedroom and the children wherever they were. The children were scared of her, and before doing anything, it was she they thought of. Would she approve or not? Was it worth inviting her anger or not?

The children had learnt to manoeuvre their way through tight situations and invite the minimum of their mother's wrath. Krishna usually did what she thought would please her mother and thus rarely angered anybody.

Rukmini did what she thought was right, even if she anticipated trouble.

Shree hung on with Rukmini because he knew it was more fun to be on her side.

X
Rukmini-Kesar Maa

Krishna would go away tomorrow. Her wedding day had arrived. The groom had arrived with one hundred and fifty guests of all shapes, sizes and vocations. A Marwari *baraat* comprised relatives, friends, and elders of the town whom one couldn't ignore. Ram's *baraat* was no exception. Each guest of the *baraat* had the freedom to behave or misbehave at the bride's house. They were no less than kings as guests and exercised their temporary position to the utmost. The bride's father had no option but to fulfil every whim and fancy of theirs.

The wedding preparations left Girdhar, Radha and Munimji physically and emotionally drained. Radha would watch her daughter elegantly dressed for the ceremonies and her eyes lingered on her innocent beauty. Black shy *kajaled* eyes, the sparkling diamond on her sculpted nose, her smooth skin a little yellow with turmeric. Tears welled up repeatedly. The tinkle of her anklets would be heard no more.

The day Krishna left Radha felt her stomach turn into a ball. Then, as if someone had scooped out a part of her and left silently. Her never protesting, never complaining, obedient girl had walked away, leaving their hearts empty.

Girdhar had held her close and sobbed—like a child. Krishna felt his warm tears on her forehead and saw Radha crying behind her veil. For one happy moment she forgot her sadness. She saw the love her parents had for her. She let that moment seep into her heart, like the sugar syrup seeped into Kesar maa's hot *gulab jamuns*, softening and sweetening them to their core. The sweetness of this moment would be hers forever.

She lifted her right foot to cross the high wooden threshold, but something made her stop. She turned back to look at her father's seat, Munimji's desk, her Dadaji's hand painted portrait, the wooden stairs, and the fountain in the centre of the courtyard. Fresh tears rolled down her cheeks.

Pusibai led her outside and made her sit, facing the threshold. The threshold symbolic of endurance and humility was now an object of reverence. Krishna sprinkled vermilion and turmeric and rolled a *laddu* inside the house.

"Our loving daughter, you have crossed the threshold of your parents never to return. Be patient and endure life's spurns silently and ungrudgingly." The women present sang the song. She had heard it many times before, but it had held no meaning. The poignant lyrics meant so much to her now.

She clung on to Kesar maa's thin frame and cried.

"Be a good child my dear, and look after everybody," she said to her granddaughter. "I'll miss you my sweet girl. You filled my life with so much joy. Now fill your husband's life with it. Go my dear go, and be happy."

She finally sat in the flower bedecked car that would take her and her groom to the railway station. The women were singing a different song, now aimed at the groom's family.

"Our daughter is young and innocent. She sleeps early and gets up late. Please don't get angry with her..."

Krishna saw Rukmini, eyes red, trying valiantly to smile, but tears rolled down instead. They had avoided each other the whole day, intentionally not looking at each other. Each understood the other's pain. But now Rukmini ran up to her sister and held her. Both cried till someone parted them and said it was time to leave.

With choked throats, Krishna heard the tearful women sing. "Our daughter is naive and ignorant, excuse any of her faults..."

Her car moved forward and the song receded slowly.

Rukmini missed Krishna terribly. She filled the vacuum with school, Shree and Munimji. On many occasions she tagged along with her father to the *chaddar* factory. She watched the weaver weave intricate patterns on the loom. Peacocks, lotuses, flowers and geometrical designs fascinated her curious young mind. She sat down on jute sacks with the women and put glue on the wrong side of the gaudy stickers and stuck them on the *chaddars*.

She visited Kesar maa more often now. Both missed Krishna's quiet presence and now each filled the other's void.

Rukmini lay flat on her stomach on the cool floor. She supported her chin with her left palm and with her right hand she turned Kesar maa's sand clock over and over again. She intently watched the sand fall in a thin stream in the lower cup. She shook the sand clock and flattened the sand. Again she watched the sand slip smoothly. She wondered why Kesar maa hadn't changed her sand clock yet.

"Rukmini, why don't you drape that silk sari and come in? You could help me in the *puja*."

"No, Nanima, I'll wait outside till you have done your *puja*. Then something occurred to her.

"Nanima, why do you allow only silk in your *puja* room?"

"Because it is pure."

Rukmini had waited for this answer.

"Do you know, how we get silk? By boiling the silkworms. How could it be pure then? Don't you think cotton is more pure? At least there's no killing involved."

"Who teaches you all this?" Kessar maa enquired sharply.

"Why, my science book says so," Rukmini replied confidently.

"It's all nonsense, we do what our *Dharma Gurus* taught us, and we don't challenge anything they say," Nanima replied a little exasperated.

"Why do you accept things which are wrong? Don't you realise God has given us brains to think and discard what is not acceptable," Rukmini knew she was making her grandmother angry now, but she decided to persist with the argument.

"That's why girls shouldn't be sent to school. Your teachers teach you utter nonsense and spoil your heads. Society will turn topsy-turvy if girls start questioning."

There was absolute belief in her voice.

"Why only girls?" Rukmini persisted.

"Because *Grahasti* is like a cart supported by wheels of the husband and the wife. If one rattles the other pulls it along safely, but if both start rattling, the cart will collapse." Kesar maa thought she had satisfied Rukmini.

"But, Nanima, why should only the lady wheel not rattle? I feel the man wheel should not rattle too." Rukmini said.

"Ram! Ram! You're impossible to convince. You'll do just as you please won't you?" Kesar Maa was looking helpless now.

Rukmini continued as if Kesar maa had said nothing. She was still talking to her grandmother from the doorway. She had stopped playing with the sand clock and stood up to talk to her. She was enjoying the argument she had deliberately initiated.

"I feel both the wheels of the cart should rattle equally. Otherwise the cart will be wobbly."

By now Kesar maa had enough of metaphors and decided to keep quiet. Rukmini sensed her grandmother's displeasure.

"Nanima, don't you think your Gopal is fed up of milk and *pedhas?* Why don't you make him some *besan laddus* instead?"

Kesar maa couldn't help smiling. "You're a smart girl, you want to eat them, don't you?"

Rukmini laughed, glad that Nanima was no longer angry.

Just then Kesar maa's cook came in with a slip of paper and some change.

"Will you tally the expenditure of this week, *baisahab?*" He inquired.

"You always come when I am busy, don't you? Anyway keep it under the sand clock, I'll see it later."

The cook knew Kesar maa never tallied it for the simple reason that she couldn't read or write.

Rukmini casually picked up the slip of paper that the cook had left, and instinctively started adding :

8 annas -	milkman.
1 rupee-	Ghee
2 annas -	Green chillies, coriander, ginger, lemon, spinach, ladyfinger
4 annas-	Potatoes, bitter gourd, sweet potatoes, cucumber, flowers.
1 rupee 14 annas	

She counted the change. 2 annas.

"How much money did you give him?" Rukmini asked.

Kesar maa thought for a second, "2 rupees, four annas."

"That means 36 annas. But, he has returned only 2 annas. Should I tell him he has made a mistake?"

Kesar maa nodded.

Rukmini ran up to the kitchen. The cook was churning the buttermilk with a thick wooden *rai*. Soft white butter floated on the buttermilk. He put his thick fingers under the butter and jerked it up and down. The butter took the shape of a ball, which he kept, in a brass vessel tinned on the inside, beside him. He cleared the buttermilk of all the butter and looked up at Rukmini who had been watching him intently and waiting patiently for him to finish his job.

She observed his *choti* knotted at the end, swaying with the rhythm of his body. He had crow's feet, which deepened when he smiled or screwed his eyes. He had big, open nostrils on a large nose. His thick moustache covered his upper lip and as he churned, he bit his lower lip with his irregular upper teeth. He looked up at Rukmini now who addressed him carefully. Her voice was alert, a little hard.

"There's been a mistake, you ought to return six annas but you've returned only two. What about the other four annas?"

He was taken by surprise. Nobody had ever challenged

him like this, but he collected himself, "Oh really?" There must have been a mistake. I must have spent it on my *supari* and tobacco. But why should *baisahab* pay for my tobacco? I'll give you the four annas right away."

He reached for the fold of his *dhoti* at the waist and loosened the change out of its tight grip with his greasy fingers. He placed the four annas on Rukmini's palms.

"Why don't you drink some fresh buttermilk?" He offered, apparently to please her.

"All right, give me some."

Rukmini returned to Kesar maa, refreshed, after the delicious drink. But something disturbed her. She gave Kesar maa the four annas and asked her.

"Nanima, do you keep the slips he gives you each week or throw them away?"

"No, I have to keep them. I give them to Munimji in the shop, because he needs to keep the accounts."

"Can I see them?" Rukmini asked.

"What for?"

"Oh just like that."

"Take it from the wooden almirah."

Rukmini held the neatly stacked slips, and sat down to inspect them.

"I knew it," she declared after a few minutes.

"Nanima, how much longer will you take now. Can't you wind up the *puja* a little faster?"

By the time Kesar maa came out, Rukmini was very excited.

"Some of his totals are wrong, but they are always more than the actual amount, never less. He takes advantage of the fact that Munimji doesn't bother to check these sundry accounts and he knows very well that you don't do it either." Rukmini was enjoying playing the detective. She liked the way her grandmother listened to her, giving her all the attention. She continued.

"And you will never know how much more he charges for

each thing he buys and pockets the extra money."

Kesar maa was surprised. "May be I trusted him more than I should have," she said calmly.

"What are you going to do?" Rukmini asked.

"I'll give him a warning."

"No, ask him to leave. Then when he apologises, give him a warning, and from now on ask Munimji to check these small things also, or better still, I will do it for you. Ask the cook to return the money to me each week, not you."

The cook was called, at first he protested but when Kesar maa asked him to pack his bags and leave, he pleaded.

"Oh! Please don't do that. My children back in Rajasthan will starve. Have pity on me this time, I promise never to cheat again."

He beat his head with his hands and said, "I have sinned by cheating a pious lady like you who fed me and my children. God will punish me for this." He cried and repented.

The drama ended when Kesar maa warned him and let him go.

Kesar maa was pleased with Rukmini's presence of mind. She rubbed her back and said, "I'll have to make the *besan laddus* after all." Rukmini looked straight into her grandmother's eyes. There was obvious pride in them.

"You know Nanima, he would never have cheated you if you had been educated. So, never say that girls shouldn't go to school."

Kesar maa had no words. She couldn't find an appropriate response to give to her spirited granddaughter.

Krishna missed her "home," her parents, sister and grandmother. There was everything there except unconditional love and acceptance. She missed her father's reassuring words and her sister's exuberance. She longed to hide her face in Kesar maa's soft cotton sari, which smelt of rose *itr* she put on Gopal.

She longed to feel her mother's fingers oiling her thick black hair. She realised now the comfort in Radha's discipline. She felt lonely, and abandoned. She wanted to be with people whom she loved and who loved her. She felt like a stranger here and couldn't relate to anyone. She feared everybody, including her husband.

Her husband was in high school and still played with his friends, while she already had responsibilities.

She avoided any discussions with her husband but was angry when he told her he would leave for Poona to study engineering. She meekly voiced her apprehensions.

"What would I do without you? After all I am married to you, not your whole family."

Ram had no answer. He left her behind and went away.

Rukmini was at school one day when Bhima appeared at the door. He whispered something in her teacher's ears. Rukmini was asked to go home. As she walked along with Bhima, Rukmini felt her heart beat faster.

"Was something wrong at home, is someone ill Bhima?"

He kept his straight face intact. Rukmini grew anxious, and then angry.

"Bhima," she said, "can't you say something?"

"Your mother has asked me not to tell you anything."

"Why?"

"Because then you won't come home."

Rukmini decided to keep quiet till they reached home. She looked up at Bhima as she walked silently beside him.

"He's so aptly named," she thought. "The Bhima in the *Mahabharat* must have been just like him." The thought brought a smile on her face.

Bhima was very tall and very dark, nearly black. He turned shiny black when hard work brought the sweat out on his skin. He had thick strong arms and legs with fat, prominent veins that popped up from beneath his skin. He never wore any footwear, so he had rough, cracked feet. He was on them from dawn to night, working in the house tirelessly.

The only time when Bhima lost his temper was when somebody else did his share of work. Then he muttered angrily and loudly, talking to himself. He threatened to give up the job and leave if his services were not wanted, he would say, to no one in particular, but for everyone to hear.

Everyone knew he would calm down soon, so they let him be.

Only Jagannath could ask him to rest, though he had to do it very tactfully.

His vigilant, bulging eyes seemed to look in all directions, missing nothing. The household couldn't function without his efficient services.

Rukmini rushed into the house. Everything seemed quite normal. Girdhar was talking to a tall gentleman with a crisp white turban. Relief spread over her and relaxed her. Girdhar beckoned to her. She ran up to him and touched the guest's feet in greeting. He blessed her by keeping his palm on her head.

"Baba, why did you call me from school?" she asked her father softly.

Girdhar smiled, "Oh nothing my child, see we have an esteemed guest, he wanted to meet you."

The guest was looking straight at her, Rukmini looked at him questioningly. Why would he want to meet me, she thought.

"What's your name, *beta*?" He asked to start a conversation.

"Rukmini."

"What do you do after school?"

"Oh! I love to fly kites, cycle with Shree, play marbles, climb the guava trees, and I love to learn mathematics from Munimji. He's strict, but it's fun to learn from him."

Girdhar avoided his guest's eyes. The guest looked amused. He wasn't expecting this from a thirteen-year-old girl from a conservative family. He smiled at her.

It was lunchtime and Rukmini was hungry. It occurred to her that their guest might be hungry too. She knew how she could escape.

She turned to her father and asked, "Baba, should I ask Maa to serve food in the kitchen. You both must be hungry." Girdhar nodded. Rukmini ran with a skip here and a jump there and reached the kitchen where she found her mother supervising an elaborate lunch.

"Maa, is he someone special?"

"Yes," she replied, "but have you met him already?"

"Bhima didn't tell me that I shouldn't be meeting him."

"Bhima has lost his mind, I told him to send you up, straight to me," Radha said, as she arranged the silver *thalis* on polished wooden *pattas*. It's corners had silver flowers engraved on them.

"Why?" Rukmini was curious.

"So that you could wear a sari."

Rukmini made a face.

"Why should I wear a sari? My *parkar* is quite new and very presentable. Maa why did you send for me from school? You know I hate missing school."

Radha ignored her daughter.

They both heard Girdhar clear his throat as he approached the kitchen. Radha pulled her sari down to her chin to cover her face and retreated from the scene. She stayed within hearing range. Marwari women had this knack of disappearing behind doors, curtains and mirrors. They stood still, like a piece of furniture and listened. Quite out of sight but not out of hearing range.

Rukmini's question was still unanswered. It bothered her as she embraced her father, "Baba why did you make me miss school? My friends will tease me tomorrow, please don't do that again." Girdhar looked at his guest, who was smiling.

"I won't my child, now will you serve us?"

Rukmini filled cool water from the *matka* into silver *lotas* and signalled them to sit down to eat. With deft movements she served diced cucumber, buttermilk and mango juice, while Pusibai served the cooked food. The guest asked for Rukmini's *thali* to be served as well. The three had their meal together. The guest seemed charmed by Rukmini and kept smiling at her.

"You have a lovely daughter, Sethji, I will be proud to have her as my daughter-in-law. I am certain I wouldn't find a better match for my son."

The music in the kitchen, the clang of the tongs, the sound of the spoons against the vessels the crackling of the fire in the *choolah*, the *'thup-thup'* of fingers on the jowar dough, the crunching *papad*, all stopped abruptly. Rukmini's world fell silent.

Girdhar was not expecting anything of this sort. His guest whom he knew as a benevolent and respected businessman had called on him unexpectedly. Then gently he requested to see his daughter Rukmini.

Girdhar consulted Radha, who was a bit apprehensive. Fathers of eligible sons do not go asking for brides for their sons. They wait for fathers of marriageable daughters to request them to 'accept' their daughter in their household.

"It's unusual, isn't it? Do you think something's wrong with his son, or may be it's their financial position?" Radha suspected.

"But our daughter is unusual too." Girdhar said proudly. Radha ignored this statement and continued.

"This gentleman has no brothers or uncles, and he has only one son. I would rather give my daughter in a large joint family where there are several members living together. I don't like these one-son families."

Girdhar disagreed.

"All the better for her, she will have fewer people to please." She had finally given her consent to fetch Rukmini from school. She felt there was no harm if he saw Rukmini.

Girdhar fumbled for words. His guest sensed his discomfort.

"I know Sethji, you are wondering why I, as the boy's father should have come with the proposal."

"I have always believed that a woman can make or break a home. I am not ashamed to ask for your daughter because she is an exceptional child. I can see that you have given her an upbringing you can be extremely proud of. My son will be fortunate to have a wife who belongs to a family with solid values and traditions. I know she'll make our home peaceful. And so, disregarding all traditions, I beg you to give your daughter to me. I promise to keep her happy."

With this he held Girdhar's hand in his. Girdhar was moved by his humility and could only manage to mutter a few words in reply.

But his guest wasn't stopping yet, "*Sethji*, you are welcome to judge my son, and assess my assets, before you give your consent."

Girdhar assured the gentleman that he would sincerely think over the matter and that it would be an honour for him to give his daughter in the care of such an illustrious man.

Girdhar didn't have the courage to look at his daughter. He looked down at his *thali* instead. It hid his tears.

Rukmini stared in disbelief. She felt betrayed and let down. But at this moment it would be improper to say anything. Any protest would only be disrespecting her father. She couldn't possibly do that. So she sat there absolutely still and dumbfounded. The anger brought hot tears that scalded her soft cheeks.

She sought refuge in Kesar maa's lap.

"Nanima, I don't want to get married. Baba promised me that I could study till the tenth standard. Why do you want to send us away so soon? My Marathi friends go to high schools and even colleges. Why can't we? My friend Nanda will finish her matric and then will go on to study for the BA. Her mother doesn't ask her to do any housework when we have exams."

"She sits with her and makes her learn her lessons, where

as Maa dislikes us going to school. Is it fair ?" Rukmini looked up at her grandmother for solace, her face sad and tearful. "Please talk to Maa and Baba. Don t send me away please." She implored.

Rukmini cried inconsolably. Kesar maa's heart ached. But she knew it ached in vain. Girls had to be sent away, no matter what.

Every girl went through pain, shock and hurt and so would Rukmini. Destiny could not be changed. It had to be borne with courage and fortitude.

Rukmini cried, but she too knew it was useless. Her tears would soften no one. She prepared herself to face it headlong.

She resolved to accept it. She wouldn't let her friends pity her. No, she would never let that happen. So when Girdhar finally approved of the alliance, Rukmini announced it herself at school.

"I am getting married. So no more boring history and geography for me now. No more examinations and I can read what interests me."

Her confidence always intimidated her friends. They believed what she said. Only Nanda knew her turmoil. She knew how keen Rukmini was to study and how bright a student she was. She sympathised and consoled.

Rukmini now read and studied with a vengeance. She got hold of books, newspapers, magazines—anything readable and disappeared into places where she couldn't be found easily. Sometimes, it would be under the shady mango trees or Kesar maa's quiet home. She even retreated into Pusibai's room on the terrace. Her mother never went there and so it was safe to hide her books under Pusibai's mattress.

"Baba, I can't read what the teacher writes on the board. I have to copy it from my friend," Rukmini announced one day. Baba looked concerned and volunteered to take her to the only ophthalmologist in town.

"You must get your eyes checked. I wonder if you'll have to wear spectacles?"

Radha looked worried too, but for entirely different reasons.

"She reads too much. She ought not to. And mind you, no spectacles before she gets married. A bride with spectacles will be the talk of the town and a lot more difficult to accept in a new home."

There was so much finality in her voice that both succumbed meekly to it and Rukmini didn't utter a word again about her world growing hazier day by day.

Rukmini was barely thirteen, when she was married. She entered into this institution like any other bride of her age. No expectations or aspirations, no love, or even eagerness. Maybe a little curiosity and a great feeling of fear. Fear of the unknown. Not knowing what to expect instilled a permanent fear in them. The pain of leaving behind whatever they loved gnawed at their hearts.

The fear of inviting displeasure from Vilas's family kept Rukmini anxious and constantly alert. She never slept soundly and sat up every few hours to see if it was daybreak. The first sign of the lightening sky made her jump out of bed. She was taught to wake up before the elders of the household did. She followed her mother-in-law the whole day mostly doing nothing. Just watching and understanding the new environment.

Vilas was so much like Baba, Rukmini thought. To her utter delight he was caring and lovable. He was not really handsome. He was short and not very fair. He had small eyes, a small nose and a small mouth on a small face, but he had a large heart. He had a happy disposition and rarely got angry. He could laugh and shrug off things quite easily. He always smiled pleasantly. Rukmini realised she needn't be scared of him after all. Her confidence so characteristic of her, lay dormant for a while. It slowly surfaced as she grasped her duties and responsibilities.

Her mother-in-law, Parvati was quite in awe of her. She had expected (and even wanted) a timid and uncertain thirteen-year-old. What she saw was a confident girl willing to take on her duties, unhesitant to speak her mind, reluctant to accept matters without reasoning. She was not sure if she ought to be pleased with her or if it was a matter of concern. Since Rukmini never questioned her superiority of status or disrespected her, Parvati had little reason to complain.

Rukmini's father-in- law, though kept the promise he gave Girdhar. He accepted and cared for her. He rarely talked directly to her and Rukmini was always veiled in his presense. Still she knew how concerned he was. Subtly he enquired whether she ate properly and drank milk every day. He asked the cook to prepare food she liked and instructed the maid to get her a fresh string of *mogra* flowers for her hair every day. If she was late to greet him in the morning, he worried and asked Vilas if she was ill or unhappy about something. He arranged picnics for her with other girls her age and sent them with an escort in his gleaming black Chevrolet. Sometimes on cold winter mornings he bought hot *jalebis* from the *halwai* and sent them to her on leaf plates. It would be *kulfi* in the summer.

He pampered her as Baba had done. He was proud of her too, like Baba was.

The only thing Rukmini couldn't manage efficiently was her *ghagra* with a skirt measuring seven metres like vast waves around her tiny feet, and the veil drawn right down to her chin. She kept stepping on and tripped over its numerous folds and the dark veil annoyingly dimmed her view making it more difficult for her to see her already out-of-focus world.

Rukmini gathered her skirt, and sped down the stairs from her bedroom to the courtyard below. The women of her *mohalla* were already there, waiting for her. Each morning she went with them to the Vyankatesh temple. She let go the folds on the last step to pull her veil down so as to cover her face. Her toes caught the folds instantly, and before she realised what had happened, she fell flat on the ground. The 'thud' and the 'tinkle' made the household assemble around her. She collected herself, feeling very embarrassed. Her elbows were bruised and her body ached. Someone handed her a warm glass of milk with turmeric powder. It would be helpful for the internal injuries, she was told. She proceeded to the temple nevertheless after convincing everybody that she was quite all right.

That night she confessed to her husband that her vision was weak and she might need spectacles. She spoke tentatively, unsure of her husband's reaction. After considerable deliberation and debate in her mind, she had decided to tell him anyway. To her relief he looked genuinely concerned. The eye test confirmed the necessity for spectacles. Within a week the spectacles had arrived and Rukmini tried them on. The images around her were sharper and well defined. She simply loved the clarity, this little thing had brought into her life. But the story didn't end here. Word got around that Parvati's daughter-in-law was wearing spectacles.

Rukmini was in the courtyard with Parvati when a group of women arrived. They made no pretences as to why they had come. One of them announced, "We've come to see your 'fashionable *bahu*'. We heard she wears spectacles!"

Parvati didn't know how to react, so she maintained a stoic silence. The women, encouraged by the silence, laughed sarcastically.

Rukmini sat silently in her veil, eyes down. But she could already feel her heart racing. One woman walked over to her, lifted her veil and peered in. Sniggering, she turned to the other women.

"Come on!" She invited them, "You too have a look!"

The second woman proceeded towards Rukmini and stared inside. "Does the *chashma* make you more beautiful?" She enquired.

Rukmini swallowed the humiliation and the anger. She imploringly looked at her mother-in-law to say something in her defence. There came none. Now it was the turn of the third woman. She held the veil, ready with a sarcastic remark, but stopped short. This time Rukmini had lifted her eyes, and stared back. Anger had brought the tears as usual, but there was defiance and determination in her glistening eyes.

The woman hadn't expected a steely stare. She dropped the veil and her jaw simultaneously. She laughed a short laugh because that was all she could do to hide her startled look. Then she thought hard to say something that would hurt.

"What a fashionable *bahu* Parvati, but what's she doing here? She should have been in the cinema!" she said.

Rukmini swallowed. The fourth woman smiled. Her two front teeth had gold drilled into them. The gold dots were supposed to enhance her beauty, but as she smiled now, she looked wicked. She reached for Rukmini's veil, but this time Rukmini withdrew. She lifted her veil off her face and threw it over her head, revealing her flushed face, and her tearful eyes. Her face said it all.

"You don't have to pick up my veil now, here I am, for you to gape at." She didn't utter a word, but the woman recoiled, stunned. She withdrew and joined her herd. The chattering women fell silent and left without another word.

A triumphant Rukmini looked at her mother-in-law for obvious signs of displeasure, but Parvati was still trying to figure out what exactly had happened. Rukmini left the room, but never veiled her face again and wore her spectacles constantly. No women ever dared to say anything to her. They let her be. Obviously, word had spread again.

Rukmini settled into domesticity, visiting her parents, Shree and Krishna.

Ram had left Krishna behind and was pursuing a degree in engineering in the USA. Marwari men rarely educated themselves, so the few men who did leave the shores, were given an enthusiastic "send off". The whole town celebrated the event by hosting lunches and dinners. Half the town was present at the railway station when Ram went to Mumbai to board a ship. He didn't realise that he was leaving behind a wife who would be lonely and miserable and a business, which would go into the doldrums due to poor management.

Never a fighter, Krishna faced all the miseries of a woman whose husband was away, with quiet dignity. She was a good girl.

Rukmini understood her sister's plight and sympathised with her. Krishna confided in her sister that their family business of silk was running at a loss. Their jewellery was being gradually sold and that her brother-in-law couldn't handle the business. Rukmini was agitated.

"But don't you say something?" She asked.

"Say what?" Krishna retorted.

"That selling jewellery is not going to help. What you need is proper management and curtailing those useless expenditures. Why don't you suggest firing those people in business who don't show results? You have a retinue of servants at home and your shop. Do you really need them?" Rukmini asked.

"How can I say anything to my brother-in-law? After all men know better than us!"

"Then sit back and watch your jewellery being sold, piece by piece." Rukmini was nearly angry with her sister. But she contained it. She thought for a while.

"If your jewellery has to be sold, then it should be done all at once. At least you have a large amount to revive the business. If this continues, by the time your husband returns there will be nothing left."

Krishna just listened.

"You know Jiji, I feel now, that Behnoiji shouldn't have left all this and gone away. It would be pointless if everything dwindles away in his absence. We all thought a good education would help the family business, but the point is will it remain, till he returns?"

Krishna understood what Rukmini was trying to say, but said she was helpless.

"Baba can't interfere in your family business. Jiji, you will have to do something yourself. Why don't you discuss it with your brother-in-law?" Rukmini suggested earnestly.

Krishna was getting irritated now.

"It's all very easy isn't it? What do I do? Just walk into the shop one day and start advising on something I know nothing about?"

"Why can't we use our common sense even if we don't have a business sense?" Rukmini asked matter of factly. When there was no response, she continued.

"I have always felt that women think more clearly than men do. They have more common sense too. Haven't we seen this with Maa and Baba all our lives? So often I see him (meaning her husband) dilly-dallying and faltering with decisions, where I can see a clear solution, where I have no doubts at all. Only we don't believe that we can think. We have been taught not to think and question and you are a classic example."

"Ruku, it's not as simple as you make it to be. Believing in something and actually doing it are two different things."

"We can do something, only when we believe in it." Rukmini said. "Otherwise we end up making excuses for not doing it."

The hint was blatant. But Rukmini knew Krishna would not take it.

Ram returned, armed with a bagful of degrees, B.Tech, M.Tech. a Ph.D., to a country that was still euphoric about attaining freedom, but didn't know what to do with it. A common goal had united them against the British, but all of a sudden there were no issues to protest against and nobody to blame for their misfortunes.

Young men like Ram, dreamt of building a prosperous India and salvage their battered self-respect. Ram also returned when the family business had been shut down. He took up a job in Mumbai. 'Foreign returned' engineers were in demand, to fit into the growing Indian industrialisation scenario.

Krishna's life started afresh when a boy was born to her after fourteen years of marriage, but she constantly worried for Rukmini who was still childless. Rukmini hid her agony under a façade of exuberance.

Vilas lost his father and all responsibilities fell on him. Rukmini lost the father figure who had brought her to his home so lovingly.

Vilas decided to take Rukmini to Mumbai for medical treatment. The treatment left her with swollen arms and deflated hopes. Then somebody suggested Dr Shirodkar. As a last resort, Rukmini decided to give it a try. He suspected blocked tubes and said he would operate. The doctor's efforts paid off and Rukmini conceived. The happiness around was palpable. Girdhar, Radha, Vilas and Krishna all rejoiced. Rukmini sensed the relief on her mother-in law's face.

Rukmini blossomed, filling out and looking radiant. In the seventh month as the women filled Rukmini's outstretched *pallav* with fruit, rice, a whole coconut, turmeric and silver coins, she thanked God for this gift and wondered what would it be. A boy like Vilas or a girl like her. It should have her eyes and heart of Vilas, her nose and Vilas's soft voice, her complexion and... She smiled to herself. Why did she keep thinking of her unborn child? She sculpted it in her thoughts and gave it a form. She talked to it and laughed with it.

As all daughters did, she went away to her mother to bring into this world her first born. She was embarrassed to face Girdhar with a swollen belly and she avoided standing up in front of him.

Girdhar understood that his little girl had matured.

XI
Rukmini-Vilas-Ujwal : 1959

Vilas named his son Ujwal. Vilas was a dreamer and wove dreams for his son.

"I don't believe in dreaming so much, at least not these happy ones. I am superstitious about it," Rukmini commented one day.

Vilas looked disappointed. "Ruku, you are too practical. Try dreaming sometimes, life becomes happier and much easier."

Vilas could never really be the *pukka* businessman like his father and was active in local politics. He went out of his way to help his friends and relatives. All this kept him away from business and increased dependence on his employees.

His father had often said disapprovingly, "You are a son of a rich man. I was not, you can afford to indulge yourself in things other than business!"

He spoke the truth. This generation hadn't seen their forefathers struggle. They were born when their fathers had most of the luxuries, and so they lacked the single-minded dedication their forefathers possessed towards business.

Rukmini didn't approve of her husband's negligence towards the family concern.

"Times have changed." She argued. "You shouldn't rely so much on your staff. You ought to look into accounts yourself and supervise the purchase and sales. I always heard Baba say that a good businessman never lets figures out of his sight and never lets purchases out of his grip."

She was earnest but Vilas always laughed it off. He never took her arguments seriously, but his lovable disposition diffused any serious arguments between the two.

Ujwal was five when Rukmini had a baby girl. Those very Kesar maa's almond eyes with long eyelashes and the very same nose and lips. Kesar maa reflected in the fourth generation. Rukmini and Vilas were delighted.

Vilas loved to be with his two children, but he appeared tired and run-down. Much to Rukmini's surprise he had stopped playing tennis and said it drained his stamina. She was worried about the constant pain in his left arm and consulted a doctor. He dismissed it as a 'bad muscle pull' and treated him accordingly. Gradually Vilas was losing his vitality and optimism. His health kept him away from business and it suffered.

Rukmini sensed it was more than a muscle pull and coaxed him to travel to Mumbai for a checkup. The diagnosis left them shocked. He had suffered a major heart attack and his heart was badly damaged. There wasn't much the doctors could prescribe, but advised a less active life.

Rukmini was stunned. Just when they had found happiness in their children, her world was turned upside down.

She collected all her courage to face this adversity, but the fear of the worst persisted. She deliberately put her fears out of her conscious mind and worked towards encouraging Vilas. However she couldn't help noticing the immense effort he now needed for mundane routine things. His staff would assemble at home whenever he felt unwell and Rukmini listened to their discussions. She offered to help him, so that it would put less strain on him.

"Let me learn a few things from Murlikaka," she gently broached the subject. Murlikaka was their most trusted manager.

"How could you help me? " asked Vilas a little irritated. "What do you know about business? It's not like medicine, which you shove down the throat and it starts working. You just cannot decide one fine day and say, 'All right, now teach me business.' "

Vilas looked agitated, so Rukmini kept quiet. Though she didn't believe a word of what he said. But she didn't want to agitate him further.

Vilas turned to his children for solace. He tried hard to keep cheerful and maintain a normal routine. He met his friends and helped then in any way he could. His popularity rose but his health steadily declined. Vilas's mother, very anxious and worried about her son's health, died in her sleep, very quietly.

Just three months after her death, Vilas came home with excruciating pain in his chest. Rukmini knew it was serious. He called for his children, Ujwal now nine and Urvashi three. He touched their faces and kissed their foreheads. His fingers ruffled their curly hair, eyes moist. For the first time Ujwal saw pain in his father's eyes. He sensed that something was dreadfully wrong. He clutched his father's palm, while Urvashi put her head on his chest and listened to his heart.

Slowly Ujwal felt his father's grip loosen and Urvashi felt the rhythm of his heart go steadily fainter. Then she couldn't hear it any longer. She didn't understand what was wrong, but the beat, which reassured her, was there no more. She lifted her head and stared at her father's quiet face. Both were sitting in silence, when their mother entered, with a doctor following her. It was all over. Rukmini stood motionless, sans reaction.

There were no tears in her stony eyes. It was only after Krishna arrived that she put her head in her lap and cried till Krishna's sari was wet.

Gradually, reality sank in. The loneliness and the enormous task of bringing up two young children. She felt cheated and let down. How could he leave her and go away? How could he dream and then not realise them? Questions arose and remained unanswered. He had been unfair and selfish. Why didn't he think of her?

Girdhar and Radha were shattered. Their stomachs churned and hearts broke when they saw their lovely Rukmini in a crumpled, unstarched white sari.

Oh! Where was their beautiful, spirited, confident daughter? This couldn't be her. Unsure, and broken. No this couldn't possibly be her. They looked away from her, unable to look at her any more. What was in store for her, they wondered? They had wished her the heaven and the stars, not this! Certainly not this! She didn't deserve this. It was unfair, unjust.

Kesar maa saw the devastation on her granddaughter's face and shrank further into her shell. She had no words to console her. She just held her close to her heart and prayed. She asked her Gopal to give her strength and courage.

The relatives left. Only Girdhar and Shree remained to sort out business matters. There was no one at the helm and both were worried. They waited till Rukmini had collected herself enough to talk rationally.

Tentatively they broached the subject. "What do you think? Should the business continue?"

Rukimini looked up. The bright eyes red and swollen, their lusture lost, the brightness dimmed. Despair all over her face, Oh! My god! Shree thought, was this his sister?

The one who led him into the orchards and up the guava trees. Was this the one who fought for him and Jiji, the bright girl who gradually carved a place for herself in everybody's hearts! So devastated? His heart melted, and the sadness dripped into each organ, each pore of his body. He hated to see her this way.

Girdhar felt a lump in his throat—he could never talk to her without choking. She just looked questioningly at them. Shree knew she hadn't given it a thought yet.

Shree continued, "Establishments in so many places and now nobody..." Shree couldn't complete his sentence. Rukmini was looking straight at him now.

"Baba and I were thinking," he looked at Girdhar, if he could explain further. But Girdhar looked down. Shree knew he would have to explain it to her himself.

"We think, you should wind up everything, sell all the property at different places and create a consolidated fund. Your expenditures can be met by the interest you will get from the fund. You have yet to collect yourself and look after your children. They need your love and attention, I think this is the only option you have right now. At least you will not have to worry about your finances till your children grow up." Shree finished finally. It had been difficult for him because he knew what it was to ask a Marwari to wind up a running business. It was humiliating and degrading.

"I haven't decided anything yet. Give me one or two days," Rukmini replied simply.

"Baba," she continued, "I would like to meet Murlikaka alone. Can you arrange it for me?" Girdhar nodded in assurance.

Rukmini's mind was in a turmoil. Shree may have been right, but something seemed dreadfully wrong. Her father-in-law had built a sound business with his grit and far sightedness. Her husband had carried it on. Would it be right on her part to dispose of it, without a thought? Without feeling the pain? She knew it was right if she was feeling so much pain even at the thought of it. Something would have been wrong if she hadn't felt anything. Vilas would be hurt, wherever he was. She knew that. She couldn't hurt him. She thought and tears rolled down her cheeks. Vilas had dreamt to give his children a sound business empire.

She hated the feeling of helplessness that was creeping into her. She was not used to this feeling and she desperately tried to ignore it. But it persisted.

She returned to her thoughts. Couldn't she do for her children what Vilas would have done? She debated over and over again and finally before the night was over, she had an answer. She slept for a while.

Girdhar and Shree sat on a *duree* opposite Rukmini. She sat on a small, square carpet made of wool. Since Vilas's death, Rukmini had slept on a thin mattress and sat the whole day in a corner on this small square carpet. Her knees and back ached as she sat day after day, meeting people who came to condole.

She addressed her father and Shree jointly.

"Last night I seriously thought over what you suggested to me yesterday. But contrary to what you think, I have decided to continue our family business."

Both looked at her with disbelief. At last Shree broke the heavy silence.

"What do you know of business that you have decided to continue?"

Rukmini kept quiet.

"Do you know the risk you are taking? You could lose all you have in the process. At this hour the sensible thing would be to play safe and ensure a secure future for yourself and your children."

Girdhar nodded. Rukmini shook her head.

Finally Shree decided to break the news he had been withholding all the while. "We haven't informed you yet, but your books show a debt of three lakhs. This was because Vilas's health didn't allow him to concentrate on it."

"I came to know of the debts last evening. I have talked to Murlikaka." Rukmini said.

"Still you think you should carry on the business on your own? In no time people will start asking for their money. They will wait only for the mourning period to be over." Shree looked worried.

"I know that. " Rukmini said simply.

"Your seem to know everything." Shree was getting a little annoyed. He wanted to convince her nevertheless.

"Who will manage the affairs may I know? Who will keep the daily accounts, the procurement of material, the sales, the income tax files, the..."

" I will." Rukmini interrupted him. Shree had seen this look on his sister's face since childhood. It was there again.

It took Shree a second to realise what Rukmini had said. When he did, he didn't know what to do. He looked helplessly at Girdhar, who appeared bewildered.

"Oh Baba! Can't you make her see some sense? I fail to understand what has motivated her to take this decision. One wrong move could jeopardise the children's future, their security. What does she know of running a business and a messed up one that too!"

" I am willing to take the risk." Rukmini said.

"Chchch"! Shree was trying hard to contain his anger.

"What for? Why for god's sake do you want to take the risk?"

"Listen Shree," Rukmini maintained a calm exterior, successfully concealing the turmoil within.

"Every Marwari child begins to learn business from the cradle. He grows up around his father and uncles and absorbs things effortlessly. He listens to their discussions and learns. He sees the hard work they put in to succeed. The child is never taught these things. Haven't you sat on Baba's *gaddi* and imitated him? Were you ever taught the meaning of profit or loss? You just imbibed it because it was all around you. The thick red books never intimidated you because you grew up seeing Munimji writing the expenses on the right and receipts on the left. You saw him fretting when at the end of the day his accounts didn't tally. Then you knew the importance of every paisa, and the importance of sound accounting. Mind you, you were never taught that. Even Maa knew if the prices of cotton had made a profit for Baba or a loss. Nobody ever discussed business with her. But she knew. Because she could read it on the faces of the men."

Rukmini hadn't finished yet. Both Girdhar and Shree listened quietly.

"With the proposal you both have given me, what do my

children get to see? They will see money coming from the bank every month, which will buy them their food, education and luxuries. It will be spent, quite easily. No hard work would be involved. Then they will wait for easy money, month after month." She stopped to swallow.

"No Shree, this is not what "he" had dreamt for his children. I refuse to wind up the business their grandfather set up so that they would inherit it one day and run it efficiently. Let me and my children learn the hard way. I am prepared to face the consequences. Let them feel the pinch of losing money and the joy and pride of earning it. Let them sweat and learn to work hard. I leave the rest to God." Rukmini finished and waited for their response.

Shree knew Rukmini, so decided not to pursue the matter further. Finally he said, "Jiji don't expect me to come and sort things out for you every now and then. I don't have that much time."

"I understand that. You needn't come to manage my affairs. I promise, never to bother you with my business affairs. Come as any brother would come to a sister to see the children growing up, to give them your blessings, come just to sit and talk to me, like we always did."

She put her head on her father's shoulder and began crying. He gently stroked her head. Tears rolled down his eyes, but there was pride on his face.

"God bless you my child. May he give you courage to face the future," was all he could manage to say. He put his arms around his daughter's small shoulders and cried like a child.

XII

The Long Red Books And Rukmini : 1969

Rukmini balanced the long red account book on the small wooden desk. Like the one Munimji had rested his books on. She had seen Munimji bury his balding head in these red books. She remembered the beads of sweat turning into tiny rivulets that trickled down his face. He would wipe it now and then with his yellowing *dhoti*. She had sat cross-legged opposite him, patiently waiting for him to give her and Shree more sums to solve.

She understood now, the labour he put in. The numbers were meaningless to her then. She held those very books now, to find meaning in them.

Murlikaka sat facing her, while she wrote the day's accounts neatly. Murlikaka had hinted that there was no need for her to bother about the daily transactions. She should see to the managerial side instead.

Rukmini didn't take his advice. She was determined to learn accounting. She believed that meticulous account books were the backbone of a successful business. She realised that she would never get a correct picture of her business unless she understood those figures in the long red books. She also knew that it would be quite tedious for Murlikaka to teach her acounting.

"Murlikaka, I assure you, you won't have to sit with me for long. I will try my best to learn as soon as possible".

He smiled and nodded.

Figures had never scared her. Once again she was adding and subtracting, multiplying and dividing. Only they were no longer arithmetic sums. She learnt to prepare trial balances.

"Murlikaka can you show me last year's accounts? I want to see how much we owe and to whom."

She glanced at the list of the creditors.

"Before they approach us please forward a letter to all of them on my behalf. Please remember I will sign it myself. Let them know that we are still in business and that I am bound to repay every rupee I owe them. All I need is a year's time."

"We could ask for more time. I am not sure if we could repay within eight to twelve months," replied a somewhat anxious Murlikaka.

"That's a target I have set for myself. I intend to keep my promise and repay all the debts within the stipulated time. Murlikaka, you have worked with my father-in-law too. He had set high standards for himself, and lived up to them. I hope to transmit those qualities on to Ujwal."

Murlikaka wrote the letters and was surprised at the response. Most of them appreciated her honesty and determination. All had extended their support, some offered to waive the interest. A few wrote to say that with Sethji gone they had assumed that they had lost their money. It was very brave of her to think of repaying debts in this hour of grief.

Rukmini was encouraged. She could now concentrate on reviving the business. She sat long hours with Murlikaka, who was the vital link between the business and her. He explained and taught. She in return grasped quickly, and respected him for his crucial help. Without him it would have been extremely difficult to achieve what she aimed for.

Murlikaka looked pale one day. He appeared to have something on his mind and was unusually quiet and thoughtful.

"What is it that is bothering you, Murlikaka?"

"Uh.... Err.... Nothing much, but don't worry, I'll sort it out," he said.

"But you haven't told me what not to worry about."

"Oh! Didn't I?"

"No."

"Well. I'll talk it over."

"With whom?"

"Our business partners at Satara."

"Tarachandji?"

"Yes."

"So what about them?"

Murlikaka paused for a moment. He had to tell her sooner or later.

"He has written to say that they are not interested to continue the partnership."

"Oh!"

There was silence.

"Have they given any reasons?" she asked.

Murlikaka fumbled.

Rukmini understood.

"I think I can guess. They have doubts about my competence. Is that not so?"

He nodded.

Again there was silence and then she spoke slowly.

"Frankly Kaka, I don't blame them. Any businessman wouldn't put his finances at risk, perhaps we would have done the same thing if we were in their place."

The elder wasn't convinced.

"They could have waited for some time and given you a chance. What was the haste?"

"Why should they not be in a haste?" She argued. "Business decisions should be quick and timely. The wait could prove costly for them. I have yet to prove myself, you know!" She smiled.

"So what do I reply?"

"You needn't ask me everything! You know these things better than I do. I have to learn it from you Kaka. Just be careful that the breakup is amicable. Let's not argue over petty matters. There are bound to be areas where we will disagree, specially the financial matters, let's not squabble over them. They have been with us since father's times. It has been a long association, which has taken years to build. Let not the relationship sour now. Such relationships are invaluable."

Murlikaka was surprised. She was sharp, observant and perceptive. Where had she acquired these qualities? Had she inherited them, acquired them, or was she just born with them? Whatever it was, his confidence in her grew. He knew now that she would make a good businesswoman. She was quick and clear in the head, but was also warm-hearted.

He hated ruthless businessmen.

Rukmini had shown fortitude when the partnership terminated but she was in fact perturbed. It was a profitable firm and it would be a severe blow to her financially. Already her business was on a precarious turn. This she had not foreseen.

She had predicted uncertain and doubtful faces of business associates, rejection from her staff, insidious remarks from those who waited to watch her crumble. Not this. She had to confront and circumvent it. And as early as possible. Before her team lost confidence in her and she in herself.

She identified the areas where she thought she had to improve. She needed a more proficient staff, qualified enough to take on responsibilities in specific areas. Secondly they had to see that their sales increased.

Murlikaka wasn't pleased. He disapproved increasing the expenses on new recruits.

"It would be an additional burden," he said, "which we cannot afford. Why do we need more people right now?" He wanted to know.

"Because we need to concentrate on our sales now. I need a person who will reach people. Let us not wait for people to come to us. Let us reach them." She paused to think, cautiously she proceeded.

"You are getting older Murlikaka, how can you work so hard now?" I don't expect you to exert yourself too much. Moreover you are a financial wizard. Even if you teach me to handle the finance efficiently, half the battle will be won. I don't know a thing about tax management. If you apply your abilities there, we could gain a lot."

The tube light flickered.

Murlikaka called out, "Vishnu, replace this thing, it's getting old," and quietly walked out of the room.

Rukmini remained there in the flickering light, with flickering thoughts, had she done the right thing? Vishnu changed the tube light. Suddenly the room brightened.

Probably she had, she thought.

Rukmini had the new recruit in mind. A young energetic man, Dattatray. He was distantly related to her husband. When his father had died suddenly, Vilas had looked after his widowed mother and him. He had caught him on the streets playing with urchins. Vilas brought Dattatray with him and sent him to the shop. Ever since Dattabhau as he was fondly called, did odd jobs at the shop. Eager to learn, he went to the bank, sold cloth, acquired knowledge about accounts.

He demonstrated his indebtedness by working relentlessly.

A customer rarely returned without buying, if Dattatray had handled him. He managed to convince the discerning man into buying what the shop stocked. He didn't receive a salary, but his family was looked after. Rukmini decided to give him a comfortable salary for impetus. This young man's talent could be used to advantage.

Dattatray beamed. His efforts had got its reward. He was now in charge of sales.

Rukmini summoned him to her office for a discussion. He could hear his heart beat loudly and his legs wobble. He knew he had to show his brilliance and sincerity so he collected his frayed nerves and faced Rukmini.

"You know that we need to improve our sales."

Was she asking, or telling? He thought.

"Yes and urgently!" he said, trying hard, not to sound oversmart.

"Hmm, I feel we should reach the rural people who do not have access to shops. But they need the cloth. They have to travel long distances. I want you to travel extensively, penetrate into areas where there are no shops, appoint dealers and sell.

Remember their requirements are different, so take with you samples of cloth to suit their taste. Cloth that is white and sturdy. You have a fair idea of their needs by now, don't you?"

"Yes, I do."

"Fine, when do you begin?"

"Now."

"All right, go ahead but show results."

" I'll try my best."

Try, he did. Within three months he had covered the surrounding areas, appointed dealers, and sold cloth. He went back to each one to collect money. He dressed like them and spoke rural Marathi. So he was accepted easily. Dattatray travelled by state transport buses or on his Luna with a bright, friendly smile on his face and samples in his suitcase.

One day he returned from one of his recovery trips, very excited. His white pyjamas dusty like the roads he had travelled on. But he was not bothered. He wanted to talk to Rukmini right away.

She was with Murlikaka, in her living room.

"I have discovered an excellent avenue to improve our sales," he said enthusiastically.

Murlikaka slid his spectacles further down his nose, and looked from above it's broad black rim. "Why don't you discover some clean clothes first?" he tried to conceal the sarcasm under a garb of concern.

Rukmini came to his rescue.

"Never mind Kaka," she said gently. "He is eager to tell us something, what is it?"

She looked at Dattatray.

Encouraged, he continued.

"The belt I travel in has so many factories, many of them are cooperatives. There are sugar factories and cotton spinning and ginning mills and they have hundreds of men working in them."

"So?" Murlikaka interrupted him.

"They all wear uniforms."

Both were beginning to understand what he was getting at.

"I have been making a few inquiries, and have learnt that the management buys cloth in bulk once, sometimes twice a year for their workers.

"Usually they procure it from Mumbai. But if we initially quote a lower price, and 'look after' a few people, we can get a big order."

Rukmini looked pleased with the information. After hours of discussions, she looked quite convinced.

"Go ahead with it right away. I'll talk to the chairmen of the cooperatives myself. Give me their names and telephone numbers tomorrow. The next order from at least two factories should be ours. We'll build a reputation of giving better cloth at a lesser price. No compromise on quality, all right? That will help us in the long run. Let them trust us always as suppliers of goods worth the money. That's where smart alecks lose out." Rukmani was equally excited.

You'll be representing our firm outside the shop, do think of its reputation before you make a deal or take any decisions. Remember if you compromise or cut corners, no one is going to give you business again, do you understand?"

"So you think I'll be able to do it?"

Dattatray was surprised that Rukmini was so enthusiastic.

"Absolutely." She said reassuringly. Murlikaka had been

silent all the while. Rukmini knew why.

She turned to Dattatray.

"You are young and energetic. But you can only accomplish your targets with Murlikaka's guidance and experience. Consult him and rely on his experience. We both have a lot to learn from him."

"Of course, any time, I'll be always there." Murlikaka muttered. "In fact, I was going talk to you right after this meeting."

Dattatray was relieved. "I want to know more about the material we can get from Mumbai, and our pricing policy."

Murlikaka looked relaxed now, he was smiling. Rukmini left them alone. The children would be back from school. She went to receive them.

The chairman was puzzled. It was rare for a woman to call him during business hours. Women had no role to play in this male dominated sugar factory cooperative. Rukmini introduced herself as a dealer in cloth. There was silence at the other end. When she mentioned her father-in-law's name, there was recognition.

Oh yes! He had heard about him. Well, she was now looking after the business. Would he be able to meet her representative?

Curiosity, at the other end.

"Why not?" He would be pleased to.

"Send him."

For the first time Dattatray was nervous dealing with a customer. If he could convince this man he could prove himself to Murlikaka. He hoped he was on the right track.

The chairman's face was immobile and expressionless. He kept playing with the glass paper weight on his desk. It left Dattatray impatient and wondering how his offer had affected him.

Then suddenly he asked. "Tell me, this lady, who spoke to me, does she really look after the business or is she only the facade?"

It was an unexpected query, it took him a second to recover. He saw an excellent opportunity to talk about themselves. Which he otherwise couldn't.

"Oh no! She's very much the decision maker, she's dynamic and is determined."

"But you are inexperienced. Will you deliver? Like hardcore businessmen?"

"Yes we will. But you'll have to give us an opportunity to prove ourselves."

"And what do we get?"

"Quality cloth at reasonable rates, and a trip to Goa with your family." Dattatray smiled, more to conceal his nervousness than feeling happy talking to the person before him.

They got the order. While the chairman went for a holiday to Goa, Rukmini and Dattatray were tackling another chairman.

Rukmini was collecting information on the cooperative movement in Maharashtra. It had been successful and popular. More and more people were buying share holdings in cooperatives. Her attention focused on Sangli. A town famous for its turmeric market. The local population had the purchasing power. They would want to spend on goods that appealed. Could that be their cloth? But how?

She consulted Murlikaka.

"Hasn't Datta come up with some bright idea?"

Rukmini ignored the acid. She knew he had still not accepted Dattatray wholeheartedly, but she also knew he was softening towards him. Both were important for her. She endeavoured to keep them both at a safe distance, so that they did not encroach on each other's domain. Rukmini managed to convert their rivalry into motivation. She remained the buffer zone. She listened and learnt from both but made sure that they interacted in her presence.

Tactfully she diffused any tension as soon as it surfaced. She wanted their best to emerge, to use their skills. She could not afford to lose either of them.

"No, I haven't talked to him yet. I thought it was better to take your advice first."

"Oh!" The acid neutralised.

"Could we ask the turmeric dealers to form a cooperative?"

His looks conveyed he didn't understand.

Rukmini explained.

"If they start a cooperative bazaar, where the shareholders can buy things at the lowest possible prices..."

"Things like?"

"Our cloth."

Murlikaka thought for a moment.

"You mean shops like the sugar industries have for their workers?"

"Yes like that, but this could be open for all. The shareholders get dividends and extra profits."

Murlikaka was sceptical. "It's a distant idea, but there is no harm in trying. First of all I'll have to arrange a meeting for you."

"Yes, as soon as possible. I feel there is potential here."

Her prediction proved correct. The cooperative was formed and it became a success story for many more to emulate.

She sold cloth in bulk, which was resold at a reasonable price. People thronged to buy because it sold at a lower price than in the other shops.

Murlikaka was pleased with the balance sheets.

Radha, Girdhar and Shree came to visit Rukmini once in a while. They watched her confidence return. Slowly she was picking up her life's snapped threads and weaving a fabric to hold her family together. Yes, this was their Rukmini, not very different from their little girl, fearless and composed, sure, sanguine and undaunted.

They both knew that the pain would always be there in their hearts as well as their daughter's. But seeing her coping with it made it a little easier for them.

"Tell Nanima, I am all right. Tell her, her Gopal gives me strength." Her eyes misted as she thought of her grandmother.

"I will come to see her soon."

"Of course child. She talks about you two sisters a great deal. She misses you a lot. After all you filled her days with joy and laughter."

"Yes Maa, such lovely days, we sisters will always remember Nanima for all what she did for us. Do tell her this." Rukmini told her mother. "I may not be able to express it myself, but I want her to know."

Mother and daughter talked, for hours, like never before.

Now Radha's fears were at rest. How would people react to her fearlessness? Did she conform to a girl's code of conduct?

These didn't trouble her any more. She could now love and accept her daughter the way she was without any guilt needling her mind.

She was no more a responsibility. She was now only a daughter.

Shree was astounded. It was only two years ago when he had seen his sister shatter. He was now proud that his sister hadn't surrendered. She stood for what she believed in, undaunted and proud. Like always, he thought.

She wasn't any different from the Rukmini he had played with. She was as determined now, as she had been when she had traded ice cream for his bicycle.

As proud as she was when she wore tattered skirts to school.

Unfazed as when Munimji had refused to teach her mathematics.

Nothing in her had changed, only the circumstances had.

She no longer kept sundry accounts for her grandmother but was handling and expanding a sagging business.

Girdhar had asked Radha one day, " Aren't you happy now, that Rukmini is different? You always had that grievance against her."

Radha admitted, "I realise now that God made her different because he wanted her to face these turbulent times with courage and fortitude. Not all are gifted thus. Now I thank God for making her different. Nobody will pity her now, they'll only envy her. People would want a daughter like her."

Girdhar was happy. "So you will forgive all her insolence?" He teased her.

" I am proud of it," she said much to her husband's surprise.

What bothered Rukmini now was that with Murlikaka tied down with a lot of other things, the shop, which was at a distance from her home was generally unsupervised. The trend had begun with Vilas not being able to go to the shop regularly. The staff had become complacent. She resolved to tackle this problem too.

She had not yet stepped out of the house after her husband's death. Women were forbidden to go anywhere near the places where the men sat, even in their homes, so there was no question of her going to the shop. She had to find a way out. She decided to discuss with her son.

"Ujwal I want you to sit at the shop every day after school." Ujwal had grown-up overnight. He understood what his mother was striving for.

"It's very important to be at the shop. Why would anyone work seriously when they know they are not answerable to anybody?" She smiled at him to make it sound very interesting. "You will see even your 'small' presence will make all the difference."

Ujwal would rather play after school than take on a serious job. But he agreed.

So each day, he went off to the shop with his school homework.

He came home in a jubilant mood one day. "I sold eight and a half metres of cloth today. All by myself! I showed it myself, and measured it. Only I asked Vishnu to cut it. I even made the bill." His face was bright with his first success.

Rukmini absorbed this moment, to store it in her heart forever.

"What were Vishnu and the other people doing when you went today?"

"Oh!" He said casually, "two of them were playing cards behind the sales counter."

"What? And what did you do?" His mother asked. "Nothing, they stopped playing when they saw me."

It was a minor incident but Rukmini took it seriously. She realised the need to bring the local business under her control first. She discussed it with Murlikaka. He agreed that the staff wasn't so alert.

"I was thinking if we could shift the shop on the ground floor of our residence. I can keep an eye on everything from here. Ujwal is still too young to manage a whole shop."

Murlikaka agreed with Rukmini and decided to implement it. The ground floor was renovated to accommodate the shop and Rukmini's office. The office was so situated that she could discreetly manage the shop without being obviously seen. The shop now came under her direct control.

Slowly but surely she was reaching her goal. She wrote the cheque that would settle the last debt and closed her eyes in relief. She turned to look at Murlikaka and handed him the cheque.

"Send it tomorrow," she requested as she smiled. "This is my *shradhanjali* to my father-in-law. He always believed in me. He believed that no one else but I would be good enough to be his daughter-in-law. I hope I have lived up to his expectations." She paused for a while. "But it is only because of your efforts that I could achieve what I dreamt. Your patience, your hard work, your trust in me..."

Murlikaka's old lined face softened. His eyes filled.

"Child you still have a long way to go."

"I know, Murlikaka, this was just the first step," Rukmini said.

Sometimes sadness crept into her heart and silently darkness engulfed her from within. Those were the moments, when she missed Vilas terribly. But she knew she had to look towards light. She looked at her two young children and sought it.

XIII

Rukmini-Felicitated : 1981

The slanting sun rays enveloped Rukmini in their warm, benign arms, hugging her like a loving mother. The bars on the window cast vertical shadows on her white sari. Each pore of her body absorbed the sunshine and illuminated her from within like never before. As though suddenly the sun had become generous. She smiled at the irony. The sunshine she brought into her life never came so easily. She strove for each ray, toiled for each streak.

Two gentlemen had just left. She was to be felicitated, they said.

"Felicitation? For what?" She had asked.

"For being an *Adarsh Mata.*"

"But all mothers do their best for their children, so why me?" She had argued.

"No," they had said, "Not just for being a brave mother but for the determination to beat all odds, the ability to take risks, the courage to face adversity, and to tread on less travelled roads."

She commanded respect and awe. A semi-literate woman rising to such heights? It was an ode to her courage.

Her school friend Nanda had visited too. She was a teacher in a school. She had held Rukmini's hand in hers and said,"I knew you would shine. Nothing could stop you as a child, nothing will stop you now. When you had to give up your studies, I knew you were disheartened. But I am so happy to see you achieve like you always did." Rukmini had smiled.

"See, I went on to do my graduation but could only manage

to get myself a job in a school. I get a salary of Rs 800. How many people with this kind of salary do you employ?" She joked. " So don't regret having missed school." Nanda hadn't changed. She encouraged and motivated the same way she had done in school. Rukmini thanked her with only her eyes and her friend understood.

Her children sat in the town hall, eyes moist with emotion. Both were fighting back tears as their mother was escorted to the stage. Their faces lit up with pride as the mayor placed a shawl on her small shoulders. He placed a coconut in the cup of her palms. As she positioned herself behind the microphone, the town clapped. Ujwal grasped fragments of her speech. Fragments he lost to emotions.

"I thank everybody who thought me worthy of this citation. It is with deep gratitude that I accept it. I could achieve what I did only because of unfailing support and loyalty of a few people. I thank them for their trust in me." She looked at Murlikaka and she knew he understood...

" How can I underestimate the contribution of my children? They have lived up to my expectations. I receive this award of *Adarsh Mata* today only because they have not failed me. Who would call me an ideal mother if they had not been ideal children?"

Ujwal swallowed the lump in his throat.

Rukmini continued. "The Marwaris fiercely guard their traditions, values, customs and needless to say their women. They were put under veils centuries ago when Rajasthan was under constant threat of foreign invaders. But the custom stuck and was imbibed as a social norm. But the veil did not only hide the woman's face, it systematically segregated her from the outside world, and also the changes and the progress around her. The veil was symbolic of her cocooned status, her helplessness...

"Gradually she herself believed that she was helpless. And

because she believed in it so firmly, each mother taught her daughter not to reason, not to think, not to protest. Only girls with these qualities would be happy when they left with their grooms. Those who didn't were bound to suffer. The most virtuous quality was dumb acceptance. To accept the good and the bad as destiny. To fight it, or to confront it headlong was blasphemous.

"It is intrinsic of man to resist change. Anybody who dares to bring about any change is under immense pressure, very often from the very people who are going to benefit by it.

"I could only prove my potential when conditions were adverse. Otherwise I would have remained a dutiful wife and mother. Till the situation demanded, I was unaware of my own capabilities.

"It is essential that women get opportunities to educate themselves and realise their potential. They should be able to face the world and its adversities with confidence..."

Ujwal could hear no more. Tears flowed unchecked. Murlikaka put his arms around him. Urvashi watched her mother speak confidently to an audience, which listened with rapt attention.

There was a loud applause, which brought the children back to their senses. Ujwal quietly rose to receive his mother as she slowly descended from the platform.

He embraced his mother. She put her arms around him.

No, this moment was not stolen. God had gifted it to them.

A well deserved moment of joy.

Glossary

Abhishek	:	Ritual bathing of god
Accha	:	O.K.
Anna	:	A coin worth one-sixteenth of a rupee
Baggi	:	Coach
Bahu	:	Daughter-in-law
Baisahab	:	Mistress of the house
Baithak	:	Sitting area
Baksheesh	:	A tip
Baraat	:	Guests from the Groom's family
Besan	:	Gram flour
Beta	:	Child
Bhang	:	Narcotic herb
Bhog Aarti	:	Hymn sung during offering of food
Bhog	:	Food offering
Bhoot	:	Ghost
Bidi	:	Tobacco rolled into leaves
Bor	:	Ornament worn on the forehead
Chakri	:	Reel
Chana	:	Gram
Chashma	:	Spectacles
Chatai	:	Osier mat
Chhadi	:	Rod
Cholis	:	Blouses
Chopad	:	A dice game
Choti	:	Tuft of hair on the head of males
Dharma Guru	:	Priest
Dhobi	:	Washerman
Dhoti	:	5m length of white cotton cloth draped around the waist

Diya	:	Oil or ghee lamp
Dumru	:	Small drum
Duree	:	A thin cotton mattress
Gaddi	:	Mattress
Gangaur	:	A festival to seek blessings from goddess Parvati
Ghagra	:	Ankle length skirt
Ghungroos	:	Small bells
Gol-matol	:	Chubby
Gota	:	Gold or Silver laces
Grahsti	:	Household responsibilities including the moral duties
Haveli	:	Mansion
Hawan	:	Religious fire
Jadau	:	Inlaid Jewellery
Kalapani	:	Imprisonment at Andaman and Nicobar Islands
Kartik	:	Eighth month of the Hindu Sak Calendar
Katori	:	A small bowl
Lathi	:	A wooden stick
Lota	:	Water container
Madari	:	Street entertainer with monkeys, snakes etc.
Maharaj	:	Cook belonging to Brahmin caste
Malai	:	Milk cream
Mangala Aarti	:	Hymn sung at dawn
Masterji	:	Teacher
Matka	:	Earthen pot
Mehendi	:	A herb used as a cosmetic to color the palms and feet
Mohalla	:	Nighbourhood
Muhurut	:	Auspicious hour

Munims	:	Chief Accountants
Murmura	:	Puffed rice
Naayan	:	A lower (barber) caste woman
Natak	:	Drama
Pagadi	:	Turban
Palla	:	End of the saree
Panchamrit	:	A solution of milk, curd, sugar, honey and ghee
Pedhas, Barfi or Rabadi	:	Sweetened milk preparations
Prasad	:	Offerings made to god and then consumed
Pugree	:	Turban
Puja	:	Religious ritual
Puja Ghar	:	Room for religious rituals
Pundit	:	Religious scholar
Rajah	:	King
Sethji	:	Master or business head
Sherwani	:	A long coat
Shikar	:	Prey
Supari	:	Beetle nut
Swayam Sewaks	:	Volunteers
Thali	:	Plate
Vaid	:	Ayurvedic doctor.

NEW AGE PUBLICATIONS

STRESS-FREE WORK WITH YOGA AND AYURVEDA —*Vinod Verma*
ISBN: 81-7822-000-8 Code: 0008

UNDERSTANDING YOUR BODY ALIGNMENT HEALTH AND LONGEVITY (A Practical "How to" Manual for You and Your Body) —*Harmon Hathaway*
ISBN: 81-7822-001-6 Code: 0016

MAGNETIC HEALING (Advanced Techniques for the Application of Magnetic Forces) —*Buryl Payne*
ISBN: 81-7822-002-4 Code: 0024

PENDULUM HEALING HANDBOOK (Complete Guide Book on How to Use the Pendulum to Choose Appropriate Remedies for Healing Body, Mind and Spirit) —*Walter Lubeck*
ISBN: 81-7822-003-2 Code: 0032

CHAKRA ENERGY MASSAGE (Spiritual Evolution into the Subconscious through Activation of the Energy Points of the Feet) —*Marianne Uhl*
ISBN: 81-7822-004-0 Code: 0040

ENERGETIC HEALING (Embracing the Life Force) —*Arnie Lade*
ISBN: 81-7822-005-9 Code: 0059

TIBETAN POWER YOGA (The Essence of All Yogas —A Tibetan Exercise for Physical Vitality and Mental Power)—*Jutta Mattausch*
ISBN: 81-7822-006-7 Code: 0067

THE HINDU MIND (Fundamentals of Hindu Religion and Philosophy for All Ages) —*Bansi Pandit*
ISBN: 81-7822-007-5 Code: 0075

THE INTUITIVE WAY (A Guide to Living from Inner Wisdom) —*Penney Peirce*
ISBN: 81-7822-008-3 Code: 0083

QUANTUM-TOUCH (The Power to Heal) —*Richard Gordon*
ISBN: 81-7822-009-1 Code: 0091

TAPPING YOUR INNER STRENGTH (How to Find the Resilience to Deal with Anything) —*Edith Henderson Grotberg*
ISBN: 81-7822-010-5 Code: 0105

SPIRITUAL HEALING (Doctors Examine Therapeutic Touch and Other Holistic Treatments) —*Dora Kunz*
ISBN: 81-7822-011-3 Code: 0113

FENG SHUI FOR THE BODY (Balancing Body and Mind for a Healthier Life) —*Daniel Santos*
ISBN: 81-7822-012-1 Code: 0121

UNCONDITIONAL BLISS (Finding Happiness in the Face of Hardship) —*Howard Raphael Cushnir*
ISBN: 81-7822-013-x Code: 013x

THE AYURVEDIC DIET (The Ancient Way to Health Rejuvenation and Weight Control) —*Dr. Dennis Thompson*
ISBN: 81-7822-014-8 Code: 0148

A NEW LOOK AT PAST LIVES (Deja Who?) —*Judy Hall*
ISBN: 81-7822-015-6 Code: 0156

AYURVEDIC COOKING —*Ramesh Patel*
ISBN: 81-7822-016-4 Code: 0164

NATURAL HEALTHCARE AT HOME (Doctor Mum's Quick Reference Guide) —*Kathy Duerr*
ISBN: 81-7822-017-2 Code: 0172

BREATHE FREE (Nutritional and Herbal Care for Your Respiratory System) —*Daniel Gagnon* and *Amadea Morningstar*
ISBN: 81-7822-018-0 Code: 0180

THE HEART OF HEALING (Body, Mind and Spirit) —*Caroline Latham*
ISBN: 81-7822-019-9 Code: 0199

THE ORIGINAL REIKI HAND-BOOK OF DR. MIKAO USUI —*Dr. Mikao Usui* and *Frank Arjava Petter*
ISBN: 81-7822-020-1 Code: 0201

LIFETIME WEIGHT CONTROL (Seven Steps to Achieving and Maintaining a Healthy Weight) —*Patrick Fanning*
ISBN: 81-7822-022-9 Code: 0229

THEORIES OF THE CHAKRAS (Bridge to Higher Consciousness) —*Dr. Hiroshi Motoyama*
ISBN: 81-7822-023-7 Code: 0237

SELF-TRANSFORMATION THROUGH MUSIC —*Joanne Crandall*
ISBN: 81-7822-024-5 Code: 0245

WORKING ANGER (Preventing and Resolving Conflict on the Job) —*Ronald T. Potter-Efron*
ISBN: 81-7822-025-3 Code: 0253

SUPERCONSCIOUSNESS (How to Benefit from Emerging Spiritual Trends) —*J. Donald Walters*
ISBN: 81-7822-026-1 Code: 0261

TANTRA WITHOUT TEARS —*Christopher S. Hyatt* and *S. Jason Black*
ISBN: 81-7822-027-x Code: 027x

ART AS A GUIDE TO SELF-REALIZATION —*J. Donald Walters*
ISBN: 81-7822-028-8 Code: 0288

HYPNOSIS FOR CHANGE —*Josie Hadley* and *Carol Staudacher*
ISBN: 81-7822-029-6 Code: 0296

ART AND SCIENCE OF PSYCHIC HEALING —*Larry M. McDaniel* and *Phyllis G. McDaniel*
ISBN: 81-7822-030-x Code: 030x

THE MYTHS OF DEATH, REBIRTH AND RESURRECTION (The Wisdom of the Serpent) —*Joseph L. Henderson* and *Maud Oakes*
ISBN: 81-7822-031-8 Code: 0318

PRESCRIPTION FOR STRESS —*Kenneth B. Matheny* and *Christopher J. McCarthy*
ISBN: 81-7822-032-6 Code 0326

LUMINOUS ESSENCE (Exploring the Body Consciousness) —*Daniel Santos*
ISBN: 81-7822-033-4 Code: 0334

THE HEALING HANDBOOK (A Spiritual Guide to Healing Yourself and Others) —*Tara Ward*
ISBN: 81-7822-034-2 Code: 0342

HOW TO ACHIEVE INCREDIBLE RESULTS BY INSPIRATION —*P. Vatsala* and *T. Gokulan*
ISBN: 81-7822-035-0 Code: 0350

HOW TO MASTER CHANGE IN YOUR LIFE (Sixty-Seven Ways to Handle Life's Toughest Moments) —*Mary Carroll Moore*
ISBN: 81-7822-036-9 Code: 0369

HEALING THE FUTURE (The Journey Within) —*Deepak Kashyap*
ISBN: 81-7822-039-3 Code: 0393

HOMEOPATHY FOR COMMON AILMENTS —*Robin Hayfield*
ISBN: 81-7822-044-x Code: 044x